GLIMMER TRAIN
TRAIN
STORIES

EDITORS
Susan Burmeister-Brown
Linda Burmeister Davies

CONSULTING EDITORS
Annie Callan
Dave Chipps
Britney Gress
Tamara Moan

COPY EDITOR & PROOFREADER
Scott Allie

TYPESETTING & LAYOUT
Heidi Weitz Siegel

COVER ILLUSTRATOR
Jane Zwinger

STORY ILLUSTRATOR
Jon Leon

PUBLISHED QUARTERLY
in spring, summer, fall, and winter by
Glimmer Train Press, Inc.
710 SW Madison Street, Suite 504
Portland, Oregon 97205-2900 U.S.A.
Telephone: 503/221-0836
Facsimile: 503/221-0837

PRINTED IN U.S.A.

Glimmer Train (ISSN #1055-7520), registered in U.S. Patent and Trademark Office, is published quarterly, $29 per year in the U.S., by Glimmer Train Press, Inc., Suite 504, 710 SW Madison, Portland, OR 97205. Second-class postage paid at Portland, OR, and additional mailing offices. POSTMASTER: Send address changes to Glimmer Train Press, Inc., Suite 504, 710 SW Madison, Portland, OR 97205.

ISSN # 1055-7520, ISBN # 1-880966-22-0, CPDA BIPAD # 79021

DISTRIBUTION: Bookstores can purchase *Glimmer Train Stories* through these distributors:
Anderson News Co., 6016 Brookvale Ln., #151, Knoxville, TN 37919
Bernhard DeBoer, Inc., 113 E. Centre St., Nutley, NJ 07110
Ingram Periodicals, 1226 Heil Quaker Blvd., LaVergne, TN 37086
IPD, 674 Via de la Valle, #204, Solana Beach, CA 92075
Peribo PTY Ltd., 58 Beaumont Rd., Mt. Kuring-Gai, NSW 2080, AUSTRALIA
Ubiquity, 607 Degraw St., Brooklyn, NY 11217

SUBSCRIPTION SVCS: EBSCO, Faxon, READMORE

Subscription rates: One year, $29 within the U.S. (Visa/MC/check). Airmail to Canada, $39; outside North America, $49. Payable by Visa/MC or check for U.S. dollars drawn on a U.S. bank.

Attention short-story writers: We pay $500 for first publication and onetime anthology rights. Please include a self-addressed, sufficiently stamped envelope with your submission. **Send manuscripts in January, April, July, and October.** *Send a SASE for guidelines, which will include information on our Short-Story Award for New Writers.*

Dedication

We do not know who our children will become,
what roads will open before them, which they'll
choose, but we look to them for reflections of what
we hope the future holds—a wide field of vision,
integrity, compassion, strength, and optimism.
Sometimes we are lucky.

We dedicate this issue to Erin Grace, our daughter
and our niece, who turns seventeen this month.

Linda & Susan

ℰONTENTS

$\mathscr{C}$ONTENTS

Michael Frank

Fiction is never transcription, but I did have a grandmother, and she did strike me as grand, even—especially—when I was small. Harriet Frank, Sr. was her name; she made up all the parts herself, including the "Sr." Invention has something of a history in my family.

Michael Frank's short stories, articles, and essays have appeared in *Antaeus, The Southwest Review, Glimmer Train Stories, The New York Times, The Los Angeles Times,* and a number of other magazines. He is finishing his first novel and lives in New York and Seaview, Washington.

MICHAEL FRANK
In the Bed of Forgetting

I

*J*n my grandmother's house the spare bed was the bed of forgetting. At least this is how I thought of it. Up until the winter of 1968, it belonged to Grandma's cousin Ellen, a silent, quaking old woman who spent all day crocheting, morning to night. She crocheted covers to pad wooden coat hangers, long fringed scarves, and slippers to keep us children from catching cold. She made the afghan that rose and fell over my bony legs as I lay in the bed, tracing its zigzags of burgundy, beige, and white with my fingers, unable to sleep.

Cousin Ellen joined Grandma Dora's household in the early sixties. She spent several peaceful years with Dora until gradually she began to mistake sugar for salt when she was replenishing the shaker and neglected to fill the Chinese vase with water. She set out for walks and disappeared for hours, so that Dora would have to climb behind the wheel of her navy blue Olds and drive up and down the neighborhood blocks one by one, frantically shining a flashlight out the window as she became her own private search party in the Los Angeles dusk. One day, Ellen walked through the apartment apparently unaware that she was holding her sewing scissors blade-end out and bumping into walls and chairs and the screen door, which was still torn where she sliced it, and eventually into Dora herself, who swatted the scissors out of Ellen's hand and held her stiff, unknowing body, seeing, realizing finally, that she was going to have to give up "the one truly unblemished soul" she had ever known. Ellen was moved into The Home, a long sticky ride from the apartment that took you so deep into the San Fernando Valley that people still kept animals on their land, roosters and cows and goats that ate the weeds that grew between the orange trees. She was visited every second Sunday, brought a tin of butter cookies and half a dozen skeins of new yarn, for while she forgot her life, while she forgot my grandmother and my aunt and her journalist son whose postcards were arranged in a halo around the mirror in her new quarters, Ellen still remembered how to crochet, and an arc of colorful hangers burgeoned in everyone's closets, a continuous woolen rainbow that spanned across our extended family. Pretty though it was, this rainbow could not disguise the fact that, in my grandmother's world, the punishment for forgetting was exile.

In the bed of forgetting, I was especially alert. I was alert to the nubs of yarn that rose out of the afghan, to the pattern of pink and white wallpaper that doubled itself when you stared at it too long, to the busts of Dora's beloved writers, Madame de Sévigné and Madame de Beausergent, that stood on paired pedestals in the corners of the room. I was alert to the pictures on the wall, dark spotted views of a river, an ocean, and a forest. Their subjects were the turbulent Columbia, a lighthouse standing sentinel over the Pacific, and a thick cluster of evergreens titled *The Washington Territory*. I was alert to Grandma Dora's bed next to mine but different from mine, a bed whose head and foot raised and lowered at the touch of a button and whose sides were bordered by rails that looked like fences you might see on a ranch, except that they were hollow and made of aluminum. Swung over this bed was a table that moved on wheels and was piled with stacks of books, tubes of ointment and bottles of pills, a pitcher of water and a drinking glass, a pen and two blunt pencils, and a box of Kleenex in a filigreed brass container, all of which was familiar to me, although there was something that I did not know and was looking at now for the first time. It was a book bound in olive green cloth, its corners trimmed in brown leather but worn, nibbled down to the cardboard underneath, its pages mostly used up and much swollen with writing. Embossed in black on its front cover was a single word that I read not as a noun but as a verb, a command. It said, RECORD.

And Grandma Dora was obeying. Just as I had never seen the book before, I had never before seen the sleeves of my grandmother's satin nightgown pushed back to expose the loose skin above her elbow, white and webbed with faint blue veins and creased in places like a fan, and shivering like whipped cream as she drew her pen across the ruled pages, leaving row upon row of uniformly slanted words, wet words that lightened as they dried, left to right, sentence after sentence. Several strands of my grandmother's silver hair had come loose from her bun, and they floated toward her shoulders, errant stems reaching out of a compact bouquet. Her chin was tucked deep into the cushiony flesh of her neck, and her mouth was folded down at each corner, but otherwise my grandmother's face revealed nothing, only concentration, all other expressions having turned within.

She came to the end. Tapping her pen three times after the last word of the last sentence, she closed the book, pushed aside the over-bed table, and glanced in my direction. Quickly I closed my eyes and simulated the slow, even breath of sleep, but through a grid of lashes I continued to watch as my grandmother lowered the guardrail on the right side of the bed, climbed out, and opened the door to her closet. She reached down a battered dress box, inserted the book, and pushed the box back again before returning to bed. Then she pulled down her sleeves and turned off the light.

Her eyes, though, stayed open, stayed level with the prints that hung over her dresser and looked even murkier, smokier now in the dark. She lingered over each one, cocking her head as she moved across the row. When she reached the last print, she continued to rotate her head until she faced me. "I saw you, Matthew," she said. "I saw you watching me write."

My heart began to bang around in my chest. I squeezed my eyes closed, but this only made the lids flutter, then twitch. "It's all right," she added.

I looked at her. "That was my journal," she said. "I've been keeping it since the late twenties, which means, golly, over forty years. I intend for you to read it one day."

"Me?" I whispered.

"You. Your brothers and your cousins. All my grandchildren. It's not quite as important for my children, because they've lived through so many of these events with me, and they won't forget me the way you will. But I'd like each of them to read it alone, and quietly. There are still parts of my life that they don't know about."

"Do you mean Annie Wozzie too?" Annie Wozzie was my nickname for my father's sister, my aunt Rosalind. She and my grandmother were uncommonly close. My aunt maintained that they weren't like most mothers and daughters; they were "beyond that"—they were best friends.

"Rozzie knows, but she'll want the journal for other reasons. She'll want to hear me talking again." This she said more to herself, it seemed, than to me.

"What do you put in it?" I asked.

"Oh, all kinds of things. I began it in Portland, as an account book. Your grandfather and I had money once, and then, all of a sudden, we were very poor, and I had to manage the household on almost nothing. This was in 1929, after the Crash, when many people lost fortunes. I kept track of every penny I spent, every head of lettuce and streetcar ride. In October of 1930 I started adding words to the figures. 'This has been the worst year of my life'—that was the first sentence I ever wrote. It wasn't the only period I would see fit to describe with that phrase," she added, emitting a small, faraway laugh, "although it felt like it at the time. My world had crumbled, you see, and my life, well, my life felt … better once I wrote it down."

"Am I in it?"

She nodded. "I described the day you were born. That very happy day."

"And Dad?

"Walt too, yes. Not the day he was born, because that was before I began keeping the journal, but his childhood and Rozzie's too, Rozzie's too." Grandma was quiet for a moment. She lifted her right arm and rested it on the pillow above her head, a position Annie Wozzie often said she'd seen me assume. I knew that, now and then, I would awaken in the middle of the night with a stiff right arm that I would have to bring down from over my head and flex several times to wake up again. "Your aunt was rather like you when she was young. She was shy. She preferred the company of adults. I used to have to coax her to attend parties when she was a girl. I taught her how to dance myself. I rolled up the rug in our living room in Portland and turned on the Victrola. I led and she followed. I wrote about it afterward. I remember thinking it would help draw Rozzie out, but she said, 'Mamma, I can dance with you, why do I need to dance with anybody else?'"

Again Dora fell quiet. Again her eyes lingered over the river and the ocean and the forest. Then, groping for the controls, she elevated the head of her bed, lowered the guardrails, and swung herself off the mattress. Barefoot, she crossed the room and knelt in front of the bureau. Her bones cracked up and down her spine as she bent down, making a sound like the one our house made when it settled in the night. Her nightgown spread out around her, pooling in a perfect white circle, a small frozen pond. She opened the deepest drawer, the bottom drawer, and pushed aside sweaters in plastic envelopes, and felt hats with veils sewn to their brims, and linen blouses so long unworn that they had turned brown along the folds. Finally she withdrew a green cloth ledger that was almost an exact duplicate of the one she had been writing in, only fresh—not new, since it was as old as the hats and blouses it kept company with, but unused. She hoisted herself erect, closed the drawer with her foot, and approached my bed. "I want you to have this, Matthew," she said, placing the journal on my pillow. "I want you to begin recording your life the way I have recorded mine. You don't have to write every day or even every month if you don't want to, but when you are moved, when you are troubled, when you are confused or struck or illuminated by something, take a few minutes to describe it. Time is very slippery. The mind is very slippery. It has a rhythm of its own, and it conceals the past in unexpected ways. One day, you will flip back through these pages and be grateful to find pieces of your experience captured on them. You will return to the moment I gave you this book and told you to write in it, and you will thank me. Thank me then—not now."

Dora pivoted and walked toward her bed. "What about you, Grandma?" I asked. "What happens when you run out of room in your book?"

"I don't believe that will be a problem, sweetheart."

"But you don't have many pages left."

"Oh, I have enough to last me."

The curtains on the window had blown open, split down the middle in a thin bar that glowed with the cold white light of the moon. Dora reached up to yank the wooden rings closer together, and the moon shined through her nightgown, making it as translucent as tissue paper. I studied her and I studied the window and the place where the moon was now covered up. Something was not right. Only after my grandmother had returned to bed and pulled the sheet up to her neck and closed her eyes did I realize that her chest was missing its plush fleshy shelf and was as flat as a man's.

I woke to the music of a kitchen appliance, the *swish-scrape-swish* of an electric mixer beating batter. My right cheek was numb. I opened my eyes. Instead of an expanse of smooth white pillow, a coarse green field spread before me: in my sleep I had rolled onto the journal, and my cheek had stuck to its textured cloth cover. I peeled my face off the book and ran my fingers over my skin, which was imprinted with hundreds of tiny indentations and, along a ridge just beneath my eye, a line of larger shapes. I got out of bed and went into the bathroom to look in the mirror. There the shapes organized themselves into letters, and I saw that word stamped into my cheek, that RECORD.

I brushed my teeth and splashed water on my face, blending hot and cold in joined palms. Then I sat down to the bowl of cereal my grandmother had set out for me on her dining-room table.

While I ate, Dora hovered over the oven, beaming a flashlight through its tinted-glass door. After a few minutes, she slipped her hand into a pot mitt and removed a shallow pan. Sizzling on the aluminum and glistening with butter, the peaks in their dough a golden hue, were two narrow blueberry strudels. Dora set the pan on the counter to cool just as the screen door behind me swung open.

At home I would have heard the car minutes earlier, but there was heavier traffic near the apartment, and there were clanging pipes and neighbors' footsteps and the general foreignness of my grandmother's environment, so I was forced to identify our visitor from more immediate evidence—the specific pitch of her bracelets jingling on her arm and the sweet prickly whiff of Caswell-Massey's men's aftershave, which was her perfume, and by the hour: it was nine o'clock, and every single day at nine o'clock, or as close to it as possible, my aunt Rosalind arrived at her mother's apartment to perform the immutable morning rituals that had launched both of their days for as long as I had been conscious of the two women and long before.

"Matty!" she said as she came through the door, her eyes sparkling and her shoulder bag sliding into the crook of her arm. "I didn't know you were here. What a nice surprise." She lowered her cheek for me to kiss, and the Caswell-Massey came toward me more strongly. "You spent the night? Mamma must have enjoyed that."

"I did," Dora said, joining us in the dining room.

"Mamma, what are you doing up?"

"Baking strudel."

"But you baked strudel yesterday."

"Well, today I made two more. I thought I'd send some home with Matthew."

Annie Wozzie set her hands on Dora's shoulders and turned her toward the bedroom. "Back to bed, naughty girl. You'll tire yourself out with all this work."

"Your mamma's a *shtarker*. You know that."

"What I know is that Dr. Markoff said you're not supposed to be on your feet."

"Ach." This was part protest and part relief, because Dora was easing herself onto the mattress, which Roz had tidied, rolling the blankets back and slapping the pillows into shape in a single fluid gesture.

My aunt pulled the blankets up around my grandmother's chest. "Breakfast or hair?"

"Breakfast," Dora answered. Roz nodded and left the room.

My grandmother's head bisected the pillow, which inflated on either side of her, two swollen clouds nesting her colorless, lined face. I sat Indian style on the bed of forgetting and opened the journal Dora had given me. I decided to try out the lesson in perspective I had recently learned in my art class and draw my grandmother's bedroom. I began at the wall with the closets and the door to the hall. This was going to be my background.

Annie Wozzie returned with a tray. *Make beauty whenever possible* was a rule of hers that she consistently obeyed: the tray was covered with a gingham cloth and had a small glass vase with a bright red geranium in one corner and a cup of steaming tea in the other. In the middle was a bowl of wheat germ combined with yogurt and slices of banana, and next to it a slice of rye toast. Roz believed that a healthy breakfast supplied a "real zest for living," in the phrase of Adelle Davis, her nutrition advisor, whose *Let's Eat Right to Keep Fit*, much tattered, was among the books stacked on my grandmother's over-bed table.

Dora opened her eyes. "Who would have thought it?" she said foggily.

"Thought what, Mamma?" Roz asked as she set the tray onto the table.

"That little Dora Isvanski would have such a daughter as my Rozzie."

"Oh, Mamma," Roz said, taking Dora's hand and pressing it. "What makes you say this all of a sudden?"

"Seeing you ... and thinking, drifting. That's who I was just now, little Dora Isvanski of Spokane, stretched out on her mother's horsehair sofa, holding a book on her chest but not looking at it, looking beyond it, into her future. I spent so many rainy afternoons lying there, years of afternoons imagining the pages beyond the book, but I don't believe I got any of it right. Not one bit."

The liquid in Annie Wozzie's eyes thickened. "Are you tired? Is that why you're talking like this?"

"The *shtarker* is a little tired, I guess."

"You need to eat. You need fuel." Dora dipped her spoon into her bowl. "I've been reading about Colette, Mamma. She had rheumatoid arthritis too. She had to stay in bed *all* the time."

Dora gazed at Roz over her wheat germ. "I wonder how she

found the energy to write. All I want to do these days is sleep."

Annie Wozzie didn't seem to have an answer. She began rearranging the objects on top of my grandmother's bureau. "How long are you staying, Matty?" she asked.

"Till tonight. Isn't that right, Grandma?"

She nodded. "Walt said he'd come by after four." She pushed the table aside. "That's all I can manage. I'll have the rest for lunch."

"You will not. I'm making you a proper lunch, tuna sandwiches and fruit salad. They'll be in the fridge."

My aunt proceeded to the second part of her ritual. She disappeared into the bathroom and returned with a shower bench and a hairbrush. She angled her mother so that Dora's back was facing her. Then she sat down and removed the combs and pins from my grandmother's hair, freeing the long silver locks. I had seen Dora's hair loose before, but I was always surprised by its length and its luxuriance and by the way, particularly when you were sitting at a distance, as I was at that moment, and squinted and imagined a little, it made her look like a young girl, the little Dora Isvanski she had just spoken of, whose appearance I knew from the photograph in the ornate silver frame on her living-room bookshelf. In this picture, Dora was thirteen or so, but her posture or her clothes, or maybe her expression, made her seem older. She pulled her shoulders back and thrust her arms forward. Her dress was made of white eyelet with a black ribbon threaded down the front and a thicker black ribbon cinching her waist. One long yank of hair, so tightly wound it might have just been taken off a spool, inched over her left shoulder; the rest of her head was covered with a large hat, its brim wide and round. Her face was in shadows, but her eyes looked straight out at you, through the shadows and across time. This girl was not at all dreamy. I didn't see her lying on a horsehair sofa—I saw her winning essay contests and running for class office and triumphing as the lead in her school play, all of which I knew Dora had done. "She stood out, your grandmother did," Annie Wozzie liked to say. "She was a star from the beginning."

Roz began to brush Dora's hair in slow, tender strokes that started at the crown of her head and finished at the tip of the longest strands, which she patted into place to counter the static that was causing them to crackle and dance like unruly daddy longlegs. Crown-center-tip she brushed, gathering loose strands, following every other stroke with a stroke of her palm. Dora lowered her head and closed her eyes and breathed in a rhythm that matched the brushing, spreading her shoulders and inhaling between strokes, retracting them and exhaling gradually as the bristles parted and straightened and smoothed. When the stripes of differently shaded gray and silver and white were all in line, Roz brushed Dora's hair to the right and wound it back toward the center, twisting it into a meticulous bun. She took gray bobby pins from between her teeth and buried them out of sight. Then she inserted the silver combs and once again anchored the familiar conch to the top of my grandmother's head.

"This sleepiness," Dora said, as Roz lowered her back onto the pillows. "It reminds me of that other sleepiness, in Portland, after I was married. Only it's different now. It's in my body as well as my mind."

"You've done too much this morning."

"I've baked two strudels. There was a time when I'd prepare half a dinner party in the morning, work all day at the studio, finish the other half when I came home, converse with some intelligence across the table, and read two-thirds of a book before going to sleep. *That* you might call doing too much, though it never felt like it then."

"Mamma, you're older."

"No, I've lost my way. I recognize the feeling. I lost it once before, for a long, long time, and I only found it again the spring I went out to find work and you turned thirteen and first became—" these words she mouthed, but I understood them anyway "—a woman and seemed suddenly to be my friend as well as my daughter. That's when I woke up. I realized I didn't have to let life happen to me. I can't imagine what will come along to rouse me now."

"It's the arthritis. The pain is debilitating. Dr. Markoff said it would be."

A silence opened up between my aunt and my grandmother. It wasn't a casual or accidental pause, but a still quiet, a deep quiet. At first I thought it might be one of those silences engineered by adults to elude "little pitchers," but soon I understood that it had nothing to do with me, that my aunt and my grandmother weren't particularly aware of me sitting hunched over my drawing. I had completed the closets and the door and had gone on to the dresser, the prints, the windows, the busts of Madame de Sévigné and Madame de Beausergent (which I only roughed in, as they were difficult to reproduce accurately), the over-bed table, Dora's bed, and a piece of my bed in the foreground. Now that Dora was sitting back again I was prepared to begin drawing her in bed, but the silence had broken my

18

concentration. I looked up. My grandmother was studying my aunt expectantly, almost inquisitively, but my aunt was focused on her rings, turning them around so that all the stones faced front.

"Well, Rozzie," my grandmother said finally, "I guess the body works in mysterious ways."

"Yes, Mamma," my aunt said into her lap. "I guess it does."

Pausing at the screen door, Annie Wozzie told me to take care of Grandma. She had closed Dora's bedroom curtains, turned off her reading light, and insisted that she rest until lunchtime. "I'll look in later this afternoon," she said as she put on her dark glasses, reset her bag high on her shoulder, and walked into her morning. As it was Saturday, she would be making the rounds of the antique shops, most likely in Pasadena, with either Mamie Glantz, her best friend, or her sister-in-law, Aunt Hillary.

And so I was on my own for a few hours. I was tempted by the sunlight in the courtyard beyond the apartment and by the narrow, sloping brick wall, low at one end and high at the other, that tested the dexterity of a boy's feet, but Annie Wozzie's *Look after your grandmother, Matty*, was still reverberating, and I decided I had better stay inside. I went to listen at the bedroom door. My grandmother was breathing regularly; she was asleep. I turned the knob slowly, until I opened a crack between the door and the jamb, a sliver of bedroom but enough to reveal Dora's wan face, highly foreshortened, more chin and nostril than anything else. This was what I tried to draw, to capture, all morning, practicing on a second page in my new book, until the sheet was covered with images of my grandmother at rest.

When Annie Wozzie returned at the end of the day, Dora was sitting up in bed, reading and finishing the last of her fruit salad, and I was stretched out on the bed of forgetting, once again working on my drawing. My aunt bustled in with two bags of groceries that she put away in the kitchen before joining us. She had found each of us a present: a Chinese brush pot for my grandmother, "Eighteenth century but late, I'm sorry to say," that depicted a calligrapher sitting at his desk and writing, and for me a lacquered pencil box. "You shouldn't spoil me," Dora said, but she seemed pleased with her gift, since she put it to use at once, collecting the loose pens and pencils on her over-bed table, the thermometer, and the tubes of salve and tossing them all inside.

She continued to admire the brush pot, spreading out and adjusting the pens and pencils. "The pickings were good, Rozzie?" she asked.

"And how. It was just like the old days, Mamma," my aunt said, sitting in a chair at the foot of Dora's bed. "I found all kinds of things. I could have antiqued for twelve hours straight if Mamie hadn't conked out on me."

Antiquing was my aunt's lifelong hobby, "The only way," she said, "I know how to relax, really and truly." My aunt was really and truly in need of relaxation because she worked so hard. Annie Wozzie was a screenwriter, and she put in long days at her typewriter or at one of the studios, where she had several scripts in various stages of production. My grandmother used to work at a movie studio herself, MGM, where she had been Louis B. Mayer's story editor. Telling stories was the closest thing we Bergmans had to a family business.

"You've been spending a lot of time antiquing lately," my grandmother observed.

"Why shouldn't I? It's my recreation."

"That's true."

"And my money. I earn half of every dollar that goes into our bank account, sometimes more."

"That's also true. It's just that now and then I wonder whether, in order to sustain your hobby, you chose to … take work that's beneath your talent, that's all."

My aunt sat back in her chair and crossed her arms. "If you're talking about the last job," she said, "I took it to help pay for the new house."

I had finally succeeded in drawing my grandmother in bed, but there was an awkward white space in the foreground of my picture. I decided to add my aunt to it. I began with her feet.

"And what about the job before?" Dora inquired.

"It was a respectable meller. I thought I could do something with that marriage. The studio liked the material. I thought I pulled off the script. You did too, if I remember correctly."

"The script was skillful, Rozzie." Dora smoothed out her blanket. "That's not really what I'm saying, though, or what I'm asking." She paused. "You were forty-five years old a few months ago. You've proven that you can have a career in Hollywood. You have so much talent, my darling, my Mutsky," she added, using her most intimate nickname for Annie Wozzie. "What I wonder is, why don't you turn away from the movies and the money for a while? There'll always be work if you choose to return, but I really think you ought to try your hand at a novel."

Annie Wozzie continued to sit stiffly in her chair. With my pencil I was tracing the outlines of her back, her shoulder, her neck and her ear, the scarf tied to her head, then her ear and neck again and her other shoulder. When I came to her right arm, the arm closest to me, it shot into the air. Her hand tightened into a fist, and it began to make a pumping motion, a gesticulation that matched her voice. "But Mamma, I've done good work! I've won awards! And I haven't done real *schlock* for money since I was starting out."

"All I'm saying is that you might consider—"

"I'm no genius. Believe me, I know that. I'm a professional writer, and there's no shame in that. Besides, Hollywood was good enough for you, and what's good enough for my Mamma—"

"Darling, sweetheart, it's impossible to hold a conversation when you're so highly strung. It's simply too tiring." Roz's arm floated toward her lap, a kite cut off from its current. "The comparison is irrelevant. I don't have one-tenth your talent."

"Of course you do."

"Not your kind." Dora took a pencil out of her new brush pot and tapped its eraser against the over-bed table. "When you were born I knew you were going to be a writer. I just knew it. I named you Rosalind because that sounded like a writer's name to me and because of Shakespeare's Rosalind, who was so clever. But maybe that was a mistake. I feel ambivalent about cleverness now." Dora paused. "Don't you want the challenge of rendering a world all by yourself?"

"Mamma, I tried."

"You were twenty-three. You were inexperienced. You didn't trust your imagination, you wanted to earn your way—I understand that, of course, I respect that. But isn't now maybe the time to be daring? You must never settle, Mutsky. Remember, you must never settle."

The drawing had been coming up out of me all by itself, an electricity of contouring and crosshatching and shading that made the two figures, Grandma Dora in bed and Annie Wozzie in the chair across from her, seem to vibrate on the page. I was particularly pleased with my aunt's arm, which I had depicted at three different heights to suggest that it was moving up and down as she spoke. Now my listening caught up with me, and my pencil slowed, then stopped. I studied my grandmother. The sentences *You must never settle, Mutsky. Remember, you must never settle* were still humming in the air. Clearly she had been the one to say them, yet didn't the words belong to Annie Wozzie? Hadn't she spoken them to me, these same words, this same admonition, this incantation, many times? Wasn't *Never settle* one of Rozzie's Rules? I regarded my aunt. Once again, she was adjusting the rings on her hands, but she had trouble getting all of the stones to face the same direction.

"I suppose this means that if I continue to write screenplays you'll be disappointed in me," she said.

"Rozzie, darling, there are times when I worry about you. Seriously worry. It's because I believe so strongly in you that I can even bring this up. Don't you understand that?" Annie Wozzie shook her head. "Then I've failed you somehow. I've not helped you find your core. My job should have been to send you farther into your own life."

"But I don't want to go anywhere. I want to stay right here with you."

"You can't, not forever." When Dora spoke again, her voice modulated, burning the shadow off what she'd just said. "Not even for the rest of the day, because the *shtarker* needs her rest. She is suddenly very tired again."

My drawing was finished. Across the top of the page I wrote, *Get well soon, Grandma*, and at the bottom, in smaller letters, *Love, Matty*. I carefully removed the page from the journal and gave it to my grandmother. She looked at it closely, then smiled and said, "That's a very accurate likeness of this room, Matthew. A very good drawing indeed." Annie Wozzie was looking at it too, but upside down, since she was tidying the over-bed table. This was probably why, I told myself, she didn't say anything to me about my picture.

II

I saw the cars as soon as we reached the eucalyptus tree at the foot of the hill. They were wedged into our driveway and spilling into the street. The rear door of one was hanging ajar. The mood in our car shifted as six pairs of eyes were drawn in the same direction. My mother's friend Bea Gold had taken all of us—her girls Myrna and Audrey, my brothers Jeff and Noah, and me—to the beach for the day. She didn't appear to know anything, although I had noticed that she'd been smoking more cigarettes than usual. I knew. As soon as I saw the cars, I knew. I knew, yet I skirted the knowledge. I didn't say anything. I didn't think—let myself think—anything. Bea parked. We got out of the car. Bea told Myrna and Audrey to wait for her. She put out her cigarette. Then she walked us across the street, stopping at our driveway. She said we had better go inside.

Time slowed. I listened to my beach thongs click against the cement. I watched Jeff and Noah walk ignorantly forward, then not so ignorantly: as soon as we reached the lawn, Jeff's shoulders drooped and Noah bit his lip. The sun was sliding behind the acacia, glittering faintly through hundreds of oblong leaves. I followed a ray of waning light from the horizon to a branch of the acacia to the dining-room window. The back of my mother's head was folding into a sea of faces. I recognized a number of my outlying aunts and uncles, a few cousins, several of my parents' friends. Jeff and Noah and I were on the walkway now. Another few steps and we would be told. The door opened. My mother came outside and closed it behind her. This gesture, this precaution, made my heart twist. She'd been waiting for us; she was heading us off; the breaking of this news was laid out, prepared for, planned. It was very bad. "Come," she said.

We were crossing the grass now, Anne and her children. We were going into the backyard. In the next window, the guest room window, my other grandmother, Grandma Becky, stood watching us, her hands folded together, holding each other, her face worried and still.

Planned. Down to the kitchen chairs my mother had painted yellow only a few weeks before, a yellow so strong it seemed to have inhaled the sun. Someone had carried three of them outside, one for each of us boys, and arranged them in a semi-circle. Standing in the garden, my mother's yellow chairs possessed the illogic, the incongruity, of a dream, and yet she kept leading us toward them. But we were intercepted by my father, who emerged from the door to the guest room.

"Boys," he said.

He came down the two narrow steps and joined us in the garden. "Boys," he repeated. He looked away, at the hillside, and then back at us. "I have something to tell you." He took hold of the frame of our swing set, fusing himself to something solid. "Your grandmother," he said. "My mother—Dora—she died this morning. Dora is dead."

It was the equivalent of a great, noble, thriving tree suddenly shedding all of its leaves: my father cried.

He cried physically, shuddering because he was fighting the tears, swallowing them, trying to insulate us but failing, because the moment his voice cracked it was already too late, we were all crying too, in unison, Jeff and Noah and I, not drifting toward the chairs that had been so painstakingly set out for us but, like our father, reaching for the frame of the swing set, supporting ourselves with it, clinging to this scaffolding as if it had been erected earlier in our childhood just for this day and just for this purpose, to keep us from dropping onto the grass, which suddenly seemed so far away that to drop onto it would have meant to fall from a great height, to crash.

And then, in time, my tears stopped and my eyes were caulked dry; the watching caulked them, watching Annie Wozzie through the window as she sat on the bed in the guest room, keening, rocking her torso back and forth wildly. I went inside to be with her, to try to help her, although I didn't know how to or even if I could. She swept me into her arms and rocked me with her and said, "Dora wouldn't want us to cry," and cried as she said this, and pulled her hair out of its scarf, and then stopped to catch her breath, to correct her breath because she was choking on her sobs, the way she choked when she ate her salad too quickly and Uncle Abe took away her fork, only this was different, there was no fork for Abe to take away, there was no Abe, not then, just Annie Wozzie and me on the bed, Annie Wozzie shaking and rocking and me following. And watching. There was nothing else to do but absorb. I could not keep up; I didn't have any tears left, certainly not Annie Wozzie-sized tears. I could only hold on. If I didn't hold on, I thought, surely I would drown, and surely Annie Wozzie would drown too.

People arrived, people left. Platters of food, deli and baked goods mostly, swelled and diminished. A turkey was carved down to the bone, the gravy boat scraped dry.

My cousin Agatha, who was older than me and wore earrings in the shape of peace signs, told me that she thought death was only a phase, a sort of holding pattern until people could come back in another form. She had had a dream once in which she saw herself as a bird, so she knew that it was her fate to be airborne. Dora, she believed, was a leopard or maybe a lion, a creature of power and beauty. She asked me what animal I thought I'd come back as. I said I didn't know.

Friends of my parents, and of my aunt and uncle, began arriving in couples, or pairs of couples; they made formal, almost choreographed rounds of the house, speaking in turn to my father and my aunt, then spending the bulk of their visit with the sibling they knew best. My parents' contingent was larger, although there were friends the siblings shared, like Dr. Markoff and his wife Elaine, who arrived just after eight o'clock. Dr. Markoff spoke to my father in a corner of the kitchen, where he kept his hand on my father's shoulder, as if he were holding up a precariously balanced piece of wood. Elaine held Annie Wozzie in her arms for a long time.

After a while, Elaine took my aunt's hand and stroked it and said, "Rozzie, you were a terrific daughter to your mother. You have to let that be a comfort to you. It may not seem like much now, but in time ..."

"Yes," my aunt said, wiping her eyes, "maybe in time."

"I wish I could be half as devoted to my mother."
Annie Wozzie shook her head. "It was all Mamma. It was she
who made me so devoted."

"She was an unusual woman."

"She was a remarkable woman."

"To have spared her the way you did, you and Walt, to have
kept her from knowing she was dying, that was—quite something."

"It gave Mamma more peace at the end," said my aunt. "At
least I hope it did."

"I'm sure it did," confirmed Elaine.

I listened to this conversation from across the room. I was
standing next to Grandma Becky, who was sitting in our
wing chair. I didn't think very hard about what I was going to
say. The sentences just came out of me, rising up out of my
puzzlement and confusion. "But Grandma did know she was
dying," I said. "She told me she did."

My aunt turned away from Elaine and toward me. A distur-
bance was working itself into her face, though of what kind
I couldn't tell, because Annie Wozzie tamped it down, for my
benefit I assumed, before she said, "Matty, that can't be."

I suddenly felt very small. I wished I hadn't spoken.

"You must be mistaken," she continued, unable to keep the
quiver out of her voice. "Where did you get such an idea?"

I didn't want to let go of any more words, but Annie Wozzie
insisted. "Matty, answer me, please."

"She told me she had enough pages in her book to last her."

"Her book?"

"Her journal. She gave me one just like it. She told me to write
about my life. She said she didn't need much more room to write
about hers."

"You're remembering incorrectly," she said emotionally.

"But I—"

"You're confused." Annie Wozzie stood up. "You're wrong.

What can you know?"

"Rozzie, please," my mother interjected.

"He's a child." She took me by the shoulders and began shaking me. "He can't be right. He can't know anything."

"I'm just saying what Grandma—"

Becky stood up and whispered into my ear, "Sha, Mattalah. Sha."

Observing this, observing us, Annie Wozzie released me, froze for a moment, then burst into tears, great hiccuping sobs that blended together and augmented each other. "She didn't know, she didn't know," she said, first to Elaine, then to my uncle, who came to comfort her. The rest of the people in the room were willing themselves to look away from this rawness.

"It doesn't matter, Rozzie," my father said to my aunt. "Dora's gone now. What does it matter?"

But this only made her cry harder. Uncle Abe said, "She didn't know, my love. She never knew."

Suffused with guilt, I fled down the hall to the guest room. It was like escaping from an avalanche. My aunt's sorrow was too strong and too large, and I was afraid that if I remained in its way any longer, it would crush me. What's more, I felt I deserved to be crushed.

My mother followed me into the guest room, and my grandmother followed her.

"It's all right, Mattalah," Becky said. "You only said what you thought was true."

"But is it true?" I asked anxiously. "Did Grandma Dora know, the way I said she did?"

My mother and my grandmother looked at each other. "Yes," my mother said. "Dora knew she was dying."

"But Annie Wozzie—"

"Your aunt didn't know that she knew. It was your grandmother's wish. She couldn't bear to face your aunt's grief."

I didn't understand—I couldn't understand.

I turned to Becky. "Are you going to die soon, Grandma?" She drew me into her arms. "No, darling. Not soon." "You promise?" "I promise." I buried my head in her chest and left it there for a while, a long while. When I looked up again, my mother was standing by the window and staring at the swing set. It was dark outside. Beyond the swing set and the lawn and the acacias that enclosed our garden I could see a piece of the night sky. It looked as if it had been packed with lumps of coal—clouds, I realized, as they began to ripple, animated by a faraway wind. In one place the clouds separated, opening in the shape of an eye, and like an eye, the opening began to glow, purple at first, then violet, then white. The eye widened. The clouds broke away from each other, and the moon swung into the night sky, as if someone had tossed it just there, just then.

This is the image I see now, this round white moon. The more I study it, the more it seems to me to have the texture of a piece of cloth, a napkin maybe, one of Grandma Dora's linen napkins with their fragile lace trim. In my mind, I reach for this object, I grasp it. It takes me back to my grandmother's apartment. Yet when I look down at my hand I see that I am not holding a napkin after all. The material is not soft, like cloth, but brittle. It is paper. I flatten it. The circle spreads into a square. In front of me suddenly is the drawing I made all those years ago, of my grandmother and my aunt talking—arguing. The picture I remember and the moment it was made too, but memory excavates something new. A piece of stilled film is activated as my aunt tidies my grandmother's over-bed table, gathers up the drawing, and throws it away. She did not want me to have seen; she wanted only her version to last. But I find that I did see, and memory did make its record, and it is before me now, more and more of it, unspooling.

Mary Overton

*Here I am at age four, dressed all in black and
wanting to look like an artist.*

Mary Overton's first book, a collection of stories, will be published in
September by La Questa Press. After much confusion and debate, she and her
wonderful editor, Kate Abbe, have gone with the original working title, *The
Wine of Astonishment*. This is Overton's second story in *Glimmer Train*. She
teaches fourth grade in Fairfax County, Virginia.

Mary Overton

MARY OVERTON
After Life

*T*he gun was gone and so, logically, should have been most of her own head. Terrianne's first thought concerned her appearance. She used her fingers to explore face, hairline, the high crown of her scalp. Heat evaporated off skin like something tangible, like vapor, but there seemed to be no evidence of her crime.

Oh, hell, she thought, I'm a ghost.

It was night. Terrianne had stood in the snow, as she last remembered, by the fallen cottonwood. The tree had been a monster. Its collapse several years before opened a clearing in the woods where wild azalea and a few light-starved dogwoods struggled. Maple and oak seedlings invaded the ground. Each miniature tree, each branchlet and twig, stood separate and apart, sealed with its own perfect silhouette of snow.

The snow lay shallow and fresh and wet, without a shadow. Light radiated dramatically. The impersonal light saturated the air.

Terrianne had walked into the woods shortly after midnight. The sky was black, but she had not needed a lantern. She had brought only the gun, its clip fixed inside, like a stone in the cargo pocket of her parka. She had come to the woods because she believed, or had believed, that her home was among the trees.

Glimmer Train Stories, Issue 23, Summer 1997
©1997 Mary Overton

Oddly, Terrianne realized, she did not believe anything now, not one way or the other. She had feelings but they were more the memory of feelings, and they too seemed to be evaporating, carried off by the steam of her body heat.

I'll freeze solid if they don't find me, Terrianne thought.

She wondered how that would affect her and then forgot to think about it. Without surprise Terrianne became aware that the gun lay across her two open hands.

There is a name for it, she thought.

It was blue-black and oiled. The barrel and the stock made a severe, obtuse angle where they joined, and out of the intersection came the silver tongue of the trigger. It was a Ruger, a precise gun, a rifled .22 full of hollow-point bullets. Even as the names materialized, she forgot them.

Terrianne for-
got the gun. In her
hands lay a hard-
skinned reptile, so
still it seemed en-
chanted. Its silver
tongue sucked the
remaining warmth
from her fingers.
In another time

J. LEON 97-

she had been told that cold did not exist, only the absence of heat. She stood as motionless as the reptile, content with stillness. The last of her body heat fled inside to her heart and lungs and liver, where it hid, silent and insulated.

The mystery is in the trees, Terrianne thought.

She saw in the tree trunks around her the serene and featureless faces of the dead. They had no eyes or mouths. Their arms, gloved in snow, reached above them. To join these dead was a homecoming.

I have never been depressed, Terrianne thought. I have

been homesick for the other side.

Inexplicably, the thought triggered a rebellion. Terrianne had to walk. She could not bear the root-like way she was sinking into the ground. She traveled without design, her boots scooping the wet snow. She maneuvered around and under things, prickly brambles and branches and deadfalls, all of them made complicated by snow. The false light lay close to the land. The sky was black. Nothing cast a shadow.

Step by step, Terrianne watched her boots plow into and lift the snow. The step-by-step rhythm, one after the other after the other, became suddenly important, although Terrianne could not remember why. She could not remember the name for the bright color of her boot laces. They were clever boots, fake fur with black rubber soles. Terrianne stopped and took them off, first the right, then the left, and stood in her bright stockings, the same forgotten color as the laces.

They are such nice boots, Terrianne thought. I'd like to keep them.

She leaned against a tree and pulled off her socks by their toes. Wet and brittle, the stockings came loose reluctantly.

Nothing here is made, Terrianne thought.

She took off her parka and examined it, along the double-turned seams and the enormous zipper, admired what intelligence had made it. Nothing was made in the land of the dead. There was no step-by-step time in which to make it. Regretfully she lay the coat on top of the boots, then forgot them both.

Carefully, deliberately, Terrianne removed her clothing—her jeans, her Shaker-knit sweater, her thermal undershirt trimmed in ribbon, her cotton panties with the clean panty shield. She concentrated on the order in which she removed things, whispering the sequence as if in a party game. It seemed terribly important that the sweater came after the jeans and before the undershirt. The sweater itself was terribly important, Terrianne thought, using her finger to trace how it was made stitch by stitch from a single line of yarn. She was jealous of the sweater, jealous of how it could be made stitch by stitch, step by step.

This is the same jealousy felt by the gods, Terrianne thought, jealous and unforgiving as they are to the living.

She walked, naked and white and shining like a candle. She forgot her name and the names of the trees. She forgot how she came to the woods. She walked until she forgot she was walking, until she was near to giving herself to the trees, until she looked down at an unrecognizable figure, bloody in the snow.

She knelt and dipped her fingers in the cold blood, as thick and black as hard candy. She put one finger in her mouth and the blood recreated a memory. A scene from summer burst upon her, of trees bathed in hot green leaves and dust, of sunlight in mottled waves, of leaf-mold with her footsteps through it. She smelled something like fire high in her nostrils, something vibrant and hot with flesh on it.

The moment retreated, ended.

Greedily she smeared blood on her hand and put all four fingers in her mouth. A memory exploded through her. She drove her old car, the Datsun, the one she called The Bucket, drove it on some damaged road where the small, hard tires collided with potholes and gravel. Sweet, hot anger filled her. She did not know why. She gripped the steering wheel so it imprinted her palms. Its plastic cover with the unraveled lacing moved like loose skin. Sweat sealed her shirt to the vinyl seat back. Her jeans chafed. A residue of cigarette smoke filmed the inside of the windshield. Permeating everything was the exuberant, juice-filled energy of her anger.

The dream ended. She stood once more among the dead. She could not remember the dream or where it came from or why it held her so fiercely. All she knew was the troubling unfairness of it, like homesickness for a place she could not remember, a place on the other side. She put both hands in the blood.

—Toi Derricotte

TOI DERRICOTTE

Poet, essayist, and teacher

Interview

by Susan McInnis

Toi Derricotte

Born in Hamtramk, Michigan in 1941, Toi Derricotte taught high school in the seventies and eighties, was a master teacher for the New Jersey Council on the Arts, training poet-teachers for the poet-in-the-schools program there, and continues to work with young people as a poet in the schools. Now an Associate Professor of English at the University of Pittsburgh, she has published three books of poetry: Captivity, *from University of Pittsburgh Press, now in its third printing;* **Natural Birth,** *from Crossing Press, published in 1983; and* **The Empress of the Death House,** *from Lotus Press, in 1978. Later this year, a new book of poems,* **Tender,** *is forthcoming from University of Pittsburgh Press, and a collection of personal essays,* **The Black Notebooks,** *is coming from W.W. Norton.*

McINNIS: *You've quoted Henri Matisse as saying, "The job of the artist is to turn himself inside out before he dies." Can you elaborate? I think we probably know what that means on the surface—but what does it mean to you when you sit down to write?*

DERRICOTTE: Well, I think it means opening yourself to discovering what it means to be human, and constantly finding new material, new theories, things about yourself that at first you may not want to look at, not want to explore. If you believe what's underneath ties us all together as human beings, then really no matter what you find, it's a way of validating human experience. So you keep turning things up, finding a way to take what is buried and turn it into art.

Some part of the skeleton that is you, is in me as well?

I wonder if I think of it as skeleton—I guess for me it becomes skeleton when you find a form for it. As it becomes a real work of art it takes on that kind of reality for me. But there's so much between consciousness and unconsciousness that is of great interest to me: What is almost forgotten. What is intentionally forgotten—like certain times our parents, our grandparents, won't talk about certain things. Trying to find a way to bring those things to the surface is interesting to me.

Is there something deeper and wider about the things that the consciousness doesn't want to bring up than about the things that float easily in consciousness?

"Deeper and wider," meaning …?

Is there something that pulls you towards the thing that won't be remembered, rather than the thing that will be remembered? Or pulls you through the thing that will be remembered to that other part?

I was thinking about what attracts an artist to—not even to the material—but to that certain kind of energy that stays consistent. Over and above the content of the work, or even the themes of the work, there's a kind of a passion that artists have that is recognizably the mind inside the poem, or an energy inside a poem, inside the work of art. I think that's really what we like or dislike about artists.

One of the things I do—I don't know whether people can relate to this or not, and really, it's not my business to worry about it—but one of the things I do, is try to go across boundaries. I'm driven to go across boundaries—boundaries you're not supposed to go across. I can remember when I was very young, there were neighborhood boundaries, lines around neighborhoods, and your parents would tell you, "Don't cross Ryan Road. You'll get hit by a car." There were these practical reasons for you not to go across Ryan Road. But really it was something else. There was a reason you weren't supposed to go across Ryan Road that was not just about the cars. There was something on the other side of Ryan Road that you weren't supposed to go to.

It had something to do with those *people and* our *people—*

Yes—exactly.

And what we *want you to be.*

Exactly. Needless to say, as soon as I could, I was going across Ryan Road, and that just happened in lots of ways in my life. And it keeps happening.

Does this perspective inform the poems in Captivity?

Well, it's interesting, the word *captivity*, isn't it? I do feel myself looking at this tension between being held and a drive to escape and go someplace else. I was thinking not only of the words *to be captive* or *captured*, but also to be captivated *by* something. To be held. Enthralled.

This book was a new exploration for me, because it was the first time I wrote about issues of race, class, and color. The other two books really don't deal heavily with those subjects. And I think the reason why is that artistically there's a danger in beginning to write about certain subjects. Our literature in the past has been presented as aesthetically bound, as if there is one kind of aesthetic that should bind our literature together—as if there's a kind of universal language and universal experience.

In my first two books I was wisely wary about going over into a kind of material which again might put me in a captive position—held in a space and recognized in a certain way that would not let me escape it. That does happen when people begin to write about certain topics and certain subjects. Often women's issues, often issues about race or class. So on the one hand I feel very driven to explore these issues. On the other hand I am somewhat circumspect about getting in those categories.

Amy Tan says she is reviewed in a cluster, almost inevitably, of Asian writers. What she says is that it cuts her readers off from acknowledging this huge experience she thinks she brings.

Well, take Matisse's statement: The job of the artist is to turn himself—or herself—inside out. Yes, absolutely. But in some way that puts a big burden on the writer of color in terms of being comprehensible. Because frequently, as soon as you begin to talk about these subjects, your reader gets a kind of—a fear, a dis-ease—a feeling almost, maybe, that you are purposefully excluding them.

You as an artist.

You as an artist. And, of course, this is not true. You're using the material you have to get to the deeper things. In a way, for all artists, all experience is metaphor. You're using what you have to uncover the deep human experiences of life, death, birth, loneliness, love—whatever. And that's your material. But it's true that the whole question about the universal has put us— as readers and writers—in positions that hold some tension. And that does have to be worked out. It will have to be worked out, of course, in our country, as we change. As literature begins to hold more voices, we will have to change.

And do you think that this … I'm wondering how you think this change will happen. Do you think that like water dripping on the rock, the rock will eventually change its shape? As writers bring the African-American experience into the universal, or women's experience into the universal, that slowly the aesthetic will open up?

I think remarkable miracles are going to happen. For example, we heard a lot in the last generation about the anger between black women and black men. This was a big thing in the sixties and seventies. Black women were very angry, and black men were demanding that black women put down their own feminist concerns and get behind the men. It was understandable: There was a fear—that turned out to be right—that white women would get powers that black people were still excluded from. And this has happened.

We would love to think that white women and black women have had the same concerns and have fought together and have been sisters together. Unfortunately, a lot of the time black women have been excluded from the concerns of white women. And, I think blacks were saying, "You're abandoning us, you're abandoning our issues." Black women were caught in a bind, because they wanted and needed to be empowered, but they were also responsible for holding together the race, as women always are: responsible for holding together civilization, for cooking the food, for doing the rituals, to bring together the social life. And so there was this great conflict.

But I've seen something amazing happen in this generation. These young writers, these young black writers—men—are so compassionate. Compassion is always the way things truly go into revolution. These young black men are writing about their mothers, their sisters, with such love and tenderness, understanding the conflicts, rather than saying, "Choose me or them," this kind of impossible dilemma. They're looking at these women. They're seeing their burdens. And in their writing you see a new way of bringing things together.

That's what has to happen—rather than this anxiety, this anger, this sense of exclusion, that sometimes readers will express. They feel excluded. They don't understand. Eventually, there's got to be a way they can take this in—become large enough to take in what was before something that made them feel angry, and to see it in a larger sense. This is what has to happen. I think it can happen. I don't know exactly when, or what the complicated process is.

It's not always true, but one of the things you're talking about is how the separated self, the person who is excluded from the group, sees more about the group and is able to be—

Absolutely.

It doesn't always happen.

Well, I think it has to. The fact is that when you don't have power, when you have to get along with people—when you're dependent—I mean this is what double consciousness is all about—that when you have to get along with people, you begin to think like them, and you begin to move into their minds.

That is why, for example, when a person says, "I never see color, I don't think about race," then you say, "Well, isn't that fortunate? Aren't you lucky? You know, a lot of people have to think about it from the time they're two years old. They think about it all their lives, and there's a great burden to have to think about it all the time."

Even now for me, talking about it here, it's a subject that I'm not anxious to talk about. Again, because I don't want to get typecast. Because once you get over there it's hard to get out. But at the same time it's a boundary that I feel the need to go over. I feel the need to understand something about human experience that I wouldn't understand unless I began to talk about this. But also, you see, my color and the way I look brings about another kind of interesting phenomena.

You've talked about light skin being as much of a block as a door opener, that in some ways it holds you back from some parts of culture as it lets you in to others.

Well, everybody, everybody—it turns out that in a racist society, in a society where there are organized ways in which people are excluded—just look at the way some recent statistics have talked about bank loans going: You know, you can have the same amount of money, the same education, and be in the same neighborhood, and if you're black, your likelihood of getting a loan is different.

There are all kinds of ways this is codifiable, but I think

internally we're all wounded by racism. For some of us, the wounds are anesthetized. And I think that we like anesthetization. Everybody likes it.

"Don't wake me up."

Yes. I mean who wants to not have privilege? Nobody. So, that's part of the tension, whether you want to feel it or not.

There are phrases we throw around, "internalized racism," "internalized homophobia," "internalized misogyny," "anti-Semitism" …

Do we all throw these terms around? What great terms to throw around!

It seemed to me when I was thinking about internalized racism and the others, that they all play a role in the world. Not just in the culture, but in this world.

Absolutely, in the world. And as I said—going back to Matisse—these are metaphors, too. Unfortunately, the very structures that hold us together as a society and create devastating kinds of realities are also about very human internal mechanisms, maybe even normal kinds of mechanisms, that are very painful to look at. I don't understand it all myself, but that's what I'm trying to find. I'm trying to find some of the things inside that aren't so easy to name *racism* or this or that.

Why do things get put into categories? What are we so afraid of? What are we not able to accept in ourselves and end up projecting onto other people? You know: "*These* are the bad people." "*That's* across Ryan Road." "*That's* not us."

Tell me what you think happens when we say, "I don't feel the effects of misogyny or of racism. I didn't mind what that man did." What happens when we swallow it?

One of the things I've found is that there are no simple answers. People do things at certain times in their personal lives, in their family lives, in history, in evolution. People do things for complex reasons, and we can't judge things in yes/no, black/white terms. That's what it means to really speak with another human being and to get below the surface of experience.

We learn these rules and we learn these stories about ourselves: What we're supposed to do. What we're not supposed to do. What we're not supposed to talk about. What we can talk about. What we can say. In some way we are then held captive in these really *not alive* ways of being. For example, if my parents, my mother and father, did not want to talk about what happened to them in the South—well, I could say they're in denial. I could say they didn't educate me. But you have to understand the great drive for acculturation.

People have said a lot about how light-skinned black people have privileges. I think it's true. Do you know the Andrew Hacker story? He wrote *Two Nations: Black and White, Separate, Hostile, Unequal.* A wonderful book. He did an experiment in the colleges where he said to young college students, "All right, everything about you stays the same, but we're going to make your skin black. What do we have to give you—in terms of money—to make this worth your while?"

Their answer was a million dollars a year for the rest of their lives.

To make it worth it to have darker skin?

Exactly. For white students.

It's very telling.

It's very telling, because we *do* see skin, and we *do* know what, in our society, it means to be dark. We would rather not.

And there's an ideal—it's almost like you think, "Well, if I say I don't see it, then I'm okay." But, you know we all know what it means in our society. So, in a complex world like that, there are all kinds of ways people have to deal. Sometimes they don't talk about it. Sometimes they bury it. Sometimes they pretend they're not bothered. They're strong. They're tough. And I think we have to appreciate the complexity.

It's interesting. I thought you'd talk to me about consequences, but you're talking to me about how reality is just—why do I think of the word thickened?—*made broader, deeper?*

And I love it, I love it. There's a woman I've worked with—and I don't want to divulge her identity because I don't think that's right—but she was working on a story. She started out by seeing me as a black woman who intimidated her, but, when we began to talk about it, she remembered a girl from her child-hood, a girl she also felt intimidated by. And then, when we began to talk about that, she began to remember when she came to school—her parents, because of their own values, had sort of instilled in her a part that felt weak—so when she came, she was in a way looking for that match to her personality, and was intimidated. And because in our society, you see, the black person is a bad one, sometimes we find what we're looking for in that place; we go looking in that place in a way, unconsciously. And she began to write. And opened up, opened up to very wonderful and complex understandings about a teacher, a white teacher, who was the first person who validated her, and told her, "You're smart. You're great." And this white teacher also told her, "That black girl, she shouldn't go on to high school. She will never be a secretary. *She'll* never make it." Who did her allegiance have to be to? That white teacher was the first woman who validated her. So here she is, aware of this moment in time when she sees that the woman whom she admires so much is not without some pretty serious problems. And she has to kind of bury that.

That's the kind of subtle stuff that I think really makes us see this as a living—

I almost see a football player, racing down the field, dodging implications.

Yes—it's alive. It's alive. These are the ways I think we begin to accept that it's not the bad guys against the good, the bad person against the good person. It's understanding the complex web that we're all implicated in, each a part of. To begin to see, "Oh, it's this big thing. And this is the way it's touching *us*." To see ourselves in that, being honest with each other. We have to realize, again, that people with privilege have been allowed to become anesthetized, and there are a lot of things that anesthetization has cut off from them, a certain understanding that it'll take a long time for them to be aware of.

This may be an odd question, but how did it occur to you how rich this vein was? You write about issues that relate to women, issues that relate to race, issues that relate to gender as well as to race, issues that relate to pain and shame and anger. It is not a vein you will abandon for some other interest.

I think it's a perception about the harm done when some parts of our emotional life die. I wrote a poem in my first book about "Unburying the Bird." It was about going down and finding that the bird that had been buried was alive. That if you feed it, it will fly away. Years after I wrote that poem, I remembered being three years old, and actually burying a bird—

A little girl with a shoe box in the backyard?

Absolutely. And, you know—in some part of my brain—that bird stayed there until I wrote the poem twenty years later. Waiting for me to transform what was hidden—what was buried—and to give it a new life. And I hadn't realized that when I wrote the poem.

I remember, too, when I was fourteen—I was writing since I was about ten—and my cousin Melvin was in medical school then, and, you know, I admired him. He was taking a course in embryology in Chicago. He took me to the Museum of Natural History where they have the fetuses—the embryos—all the way from conception to birth. And, you know, I was like fourteen years old. Nobody had ever talked to me about these things. So I was really impressed. I just knew that Melvin would be the one to show my poems to—because I wasn't showing anybody at that time. And so I said to myself, he's going to appreciate what's hidden and buried and mysterious.

Because he has all these true things in front of him, right?

Yes. He had shown me these things. And, so I showed him my

poems and he said, "These are really sick! These are really morbid!" And the point was: I was not writing about the things that made you happy to hear about. One of the burdens that kids have is that they're supposed to be happy. If they're happy, their parents think, or their friends or their relatives think, that *they've* done a good job and they're being good parents. It's a heck of a burden for kids. That's why I love to teach poetry to them. Fourth graders. Fifth graders. There's so much of this powerful questioning about life and observation that can come out in creative work. So often it can't come out in our relations with the people we love the most. They don't want us to be disturbed. They don't want us to be unhappy. But that's just a part of experience.

It's an interesting thought that people don't want children—or the people they love—to be unhappy because it's a reflection on themselves.

Exactly. Exactly. And parents worry, you know, if their children are talking about dead birds.

But, so, in that situation with Melvin, either I could stop writing or I could write about what Melvin wanted—I mean, I would kind of know what he would want me to write about— or I could go hide some more.

You went and hid somewhere?

I went and hid somewhere.

You write autobiography, in many ways. I mean, not strictly, but in many ways. Does that give you a place to stand on the planet?

Yes, it does. That's a good way of putting it.

Some people are defined by society in ways that disempower them—in ways that take away their uniqueness. They're placed in some category of "other," and stereotyped. Blacks in our society are cast as "ignorant," even "beastlike." "Not alive." It's passed down from slavery. If the "other" is an animal, you can own them and not feel guilty—and do terrible things to them— if they're not alive. You deaden them. Okay, so here you are, this person, a part of you understanding in your consciousness that in this society you are "dead meat." You don't exist. You are invisible. You are not recognized. You could be an athlete, you know, or a dancer.

A model.

A model. Yes. You are a body. You're flesh. You're meat. You're a slave.

Okay. Now you carve out a mind and a soul that makes you unique, that gives you individuality, beauty, and sacredness—even sacredness, you see. You have to invent this. You have to invent your own life. And you have to sort of take the mirrors that have been put there—that your society is reflecting back to you—you are a nanny, the image of a black woman who takes care of white people. Whatever these mirrors are—the mirrors we get stuck in—and which a part of us believes in our own minds, because of course, we do—we do internalize. And then you have to find other mirrors, invent other mirrors in which you can see yourselves as sacred and powerful.

Very nice—to talk about it as the mirror. We do see ourselves as others describe us to be.

Right. Yes.

I want to ask you a question about the canon, and not just the Great Canon of Literature, *but the written word that we see all around us. How is it for a writer, seeing herself as a writer, in a culture that doesn't have a long tradition of recognizing and celebrating artists of color? Do you see things changing with the diversification of the canon, the willingness of—*

Toni Morrison talks about—lots of things she's talked about lately are so wonderful—about how American literature isn't complete until all the stories are there. She also talks about the need for the canon, the white writers as they exist right now—for some strange reason we have pretended they weren't touched by the racial climate of our American society. I mean it's crazy—for us to begin to look at the literature that we've read in the past and that we know very well. To understand *why*

Moby Dick, why the great *white* whale? Why was Melville so interested in holding this up as a symbol? Why was it written at the time it was written? Did it have anything to do with slavery in our society? You see, these are the things that we haven't talked about. There is a great deal of texture that's already in our literature that we haven't talked about. Once we begin to acknowledge the way we've been touched by this great force, and stop pretending we didn't know this, I think we can make some very interesting networks that will begin to pull our literature together. But one of the things that's so important is to empower people who don't know how to begin to speak about their experience because they're ashamed of it.

You talked about a girl in high school. Your assignment was—again, I think you were participating as a poet-in-the-schools—and your assignment was for the students to write about what they saw outside their windows. And she wouldn't do it, because she didn't want to write about pimps and prostitutes.

That's right.

Pee-stained mattresses.

Right, because—because it means that something's wrong with you.

Right. If I have to look out on that, then—

That's another thing we have to think about. How do people defend themselves psychically against self-annihilation—of worth, self-worth, ego? When you see kids walking around in hundred-dollar sneakers, you say they could be using that money for something else. I know that. Everybody has different values, but there are all kinds of reasons people do things just to survive—with ego intact. How powerful a drive this is when forces are very destructive against the sense of self.

But writing is so powerful, you see. People who have been—marginalized is a very common word—they feel their experience is not valuable. Okay, I look out of my window and I don't see—what?

A tree growing in Brooklyn?

A tree growing in Brooklyn. I see pimps and prostitutes. That means I don't live in a good place. That means my house is not good. That means I'm not good. That means my parents aren't good. Oh, well, I'm not going to talk about that.

I have nothing to write about.

Well, no, it's worse than that. I'm ashamed. I'm the person who goes to school in my hundred-dollar sneakers and I am always clean. So why am I going to write about looking out of my window and seeing a pee-stained mattress? People don't know me that way, they know me as someone who's always dressed well. How do they know where I live? They don't. So, I'm not going to begin to tell them that.

And as a teacher, you say to that student ...?

I would never presume to know the way for anybody. But I would say, when that person does tell me that, I would say, "You know, I'm really moved by what you've done." Because, very interestingly, you see—and the kids have to catch on to this— what they've hidden is their power. That's their power. The hidden has a kind of energy inside it, just like that little bird that I hid, buried. Somewhere—it sticks back somewhere, and a part of you knows that it has to come forth in a different way.

This has come full circle. Matisse again.

Yes. And this is the creative act, the human creative act. When the child begins to see that, okay, it looks ugly first, the first time you look at it. But you have other eyes. There are other mirrors. To be empowered to speak and to move another human being is transformation. It's a great power for young people. And, boy, have I seen it change people's lives—young people.

Emerging out through their own words, as if listening to themselves allows them to grow into more of themselves?

As if, as if suddenly being aware of—I think—I don't know. I can't answer that.

I'm thinking of a little fourth grader, Maritza Hoyas, who

came over to this country. She learned how to speak English by watching TV. Her parents didn't know. She's from Colombia. When she was nine years old she wrote this poem:

Blind Hands

Like two blind birds that don't know you,
My hands come up upon the earth.
Into the dark they will find you.
Grow to the stars, shine through the moon.
Go far, blind hands,
I'll wait for you.

She's nine.

I think you discover your language. You discover the invisible thing that is really your power.

The sneakers are okay.

But to have a language that is so beautiful … In some way we know when that language comes. We begin to understand the beauty of it, and the power. You can't take that away from somebody. That's why you could put her someplace totally alone, and she could still have access to it. That's pretty strong. Pretty strong. It feels good.

This interview was recorded for *Conversations with Susan McInnis*, KUAC-FM/TV, at the University of Alaska, Fairbanks. Born in San Francisco, Susan McInnis worked with KUAC-FM/TV in Fairbanks for ten years, interviewing authors (among others) for eight years. She'll have resigned from KUAC by the time this issue of *Glimmer Train Stories* comes out, and will be writing for a living, and working on her thesis, expecting to have earned her MFA in creative writing from the University of Alaska, Fairbanks in May of this year.

Kent Nelson

Still stubborn after all these years.

Kent Nelson has traveled enough in remote places to see 698 species of North American birds. Last fall he ran the Imogene Pass Race from Ouray to Telluride—eighteen miles and 5,314 feet of elevation gain—in three hours and thirty-one minutes. He claims he's not fast, just persistent. His last novel, *Language in the Blood*, won the Edward Abbey Prize for Ecofiction, but is now out of print. Nelson's stories are forthcoming in *The Gettysburg Review* and in *The Southern Review*. "The Middle of Nowhere" was included in the ten-year Pushcart anthology.

KENT NELSON
Night Sky Opening Outward

il drove slowly and without headlights, a little wavery still from the cocktail party at the Olsonbakers' pool. It was nearly dark, but warm out, Indian Summer, and Julia had her window down. To the west, where the sun had long since disappeared, a faint, pale turquoise silhouetted the feathery horizon of treetops. The Volvo moved through the yellow and red maples on either side with such a startling ease Gil felt giddy with power.

He followed the Eversons' Saab at some remove, watching their headlights delve into the woods as the Saab curved along the road. Julia stared out the window, as if she did not want to look at him, let alone speak, and he made his presence known by shifting to neutral and coasting down the hill, picking up speed the whole way and closing on the Eversons. Julia didn't flinch.

Tom Everson flashed his red brake lights and turned off at Trumbull Road. Gil honked at them, but neither Tom nor Marie waved, though their sun roof was open. Suddenly, without the Eversons' headlights, it was dark as night, but even then Julia didn't speak. They coasted through the pale yellow leaves of the trees toward the creek bottom.

It was cooler where the water flowed along the rocky path. They crossed the bridge, and when the car slowed on the uphill,

Gil shifted to second and turned on the headlights. Julia sighed.

"I don't see why you have to bring up politics," Julia said. "No one wants to discuss politics at a party."

"It's the only place I can," Gil said.

"You made the Olsonbakers uncomfortable."

"They deserve to be uncomfortable, don't you think? Nixon should have died in jail, but instead he's on a postage stamp."

"That isn't Marie's fault."

"She's a Republican. Whose fault is it? And Oliver North's being paid to give speeches …"

They climbed the flank of the hill and passed through the Audubon tract. Julia's chin was raised, and her nose and eyes were marked by deep shadows from the street lamp which shone from the corner of Red Coat Lane. The shadows made her face garish, as if she wore a mask. She turned away again, as if to see what the Barrymores, whose lights were ablaze through the trees, were doing on a Sunday night.

"Why do you drink so much, Gil?" she asked.

"You think booze makes me political?"

"I think no one would say what you do without drink."

"I had three ounces of gin. Is that a lot?"

"You didn't have to say you were left of Daniel Ortega."

They reached their own street, Saw Mill Lane, and Gil turned off the headlights again because he knew the way home.

They had been married eleven years, and Julia had drifted away from him day by day, week by week. Gil had noticed the change in the tone of her voice and the subtle habits she'd fall into by accident or design. She seldom looked at him when he talked; the clothes hamper that had been in the bathroom was now in her dressing area; asleep, she edged away from him in bed inch by inch. Some of her avoidances seemed natural: as she became more indispensible at the museum, she gave more evenings to her work; she had to exercise and groom the horse she had bought; she was asked to serve on committees for the symphony and the library. And her health was fragile. She worried about the pain in her foot, the nausea that had plagued her for the last two years, and twice she had been to the doctor recently about the tenderness in her shoulder.

The field at the corner shone brightly in the moonlight, and beyond it their house stood on a rocky shelf. Gil had wanted Julia to keep her horse there, but the grass was shallow in nutrients and had to be reseeded. He slowed the Volvo to twenty. In the darkness, the field gave off a misty velvet glow from the moonlight that he thought quite beautiful.

"Why are you slowing down?" she asked.

"Maybe you could go alone to these parties," he said.

"You could make an effort, Gil. I like my friends."

He turned in at the mailbox with painted laurel leaves on it, gave gas up the hill, and coasted to a stop in the apron. They sat for a moment in silence, listening to the sparse calls of insects in the nearby apple trees, the muffled sound of the creek behind the house, the hum of traffic on the parkway in the distance. "How's the shoulder?" he asked.

"All right. A little sore."

Gil leaned his head back on the headrest. The liquor he'd drunk made him keener, and he wanted to make amends. "I could rub some liniment on it."

"I'll survive."

She snapped open the door on her side. Quickly he opened his, too, and went around to help her. But she refused the offer of his hand. She braced herself on the armrest for purchase and winced as she pushed herself up.

"But don't you want to do more than survive?" he asked. He blocked her way slightly, but she sidestepped him and went up the flagstone walkway that divided the lawn and led to the front door.

He stayed where he was. The air was sweet with the smell of apples and dying grasses. He looked up into the canopy of apple trees where a sudden breeze made the leaves alive. The lights of the town hovered in the low clouds and gave that part of the sky an eerie reverberation, like an echoing noise against the purer stars over the field. Because of the lights, the moon was a pale mask. It made him sad that, no matter what he'd said at the party, his wife would not embrace him on such an evening.

"Gil?"

He turned and saw Julia was standing on the lawn. "I'm right here," he said.

"There's an intruder."

He crossed the apron and came up the walk to where she was standing. "What do you mean? Did the alarm go off?"

"I don't think so."

"Are any lights on?"

"Just the hall light. I heard something, but I was afraid to go in."

Gil nodded and went past her, farther out onto the lawn where he had a view of the whole house. It was a modest house by neighborhood standards—a two-story Craftsman. The dormers were dark; the bathroom, the upstairs bedroom where Julia kept her jewelry in a safe, were dark; the kitchen was dark. Nothing was out of the ordinary that he could see. No lights were on anywhere except the one they always left on in the front foyer.

He stepped across the grass toward the front door.

"Be careful," Julia said.

"I am left of Daniel Ortega," he said.

The doorway was ground level, and as he paused under the eave, he sensed for the first time the gin he had drunk at the Olsonbakers' pool. He felt heightened courage, an awareness of everything around him—the shadows, the silence, Julia standing behind him on the lawn. He looked through the small panes of glass beside the front door, saw the lamp they'd left on, the

54

Oriental rug in the foyer, and above the secretary the painting of the brigantine on high seas. Next to it, the tiny red light of the burglar alarm was still on. He didn't hear anything.

He fitted his key and opened the door. Immediately the alarm system beeped, and he crossed the foyer and punched in the code. The alarm switched off.

He listened to the house. There was something—a noise in the living room.

"What is it?" Julia asked.

Her voice startled him. She had come inside the door.

"Shhh."

"Do you hear anything?"

A brief flurry of sound, almost like a whisper, came from the living room, then a thudding noise, and the flurry again. Gil went into the living room and switched on the chandelier.

The bird fluttered for a moment against its own reflection in the plate-glass window—the darkness beyond—then flew toward the light. It was a small falcon, a foot long, maybe a little more, with a slate blue back, a barred orange tail, and black markings on its head.

"It must have come down the chimney," Julia said. "At least it's not a burglar."

Gil skirted the sofa and winched open the two windows in the corner of the room. The chiffon curtains beside them lufted in the breeze.

"The curtains will scare it," Julia said.

The bird circled the chandelier, then landed on the back of a wingback chair near the fireplace. *The Art of the Prado* lay on the coffee table in front of the sofa. Gil pulled the curtains back and fixed them to the window frame. "I wonder what kind of bird it is. Marie Everson would know. Maybe I should call her."

Julia smiled, though she tried not to. "You can call her and apologize," Julia said.

Gil looked at the bird more closely—what did it know about its own odd predicament? A black mark like a teardrop bled through its fierce eye and down the side of its face.

"You think it would smell the air," Julia said, "or feel it moving."

"Maybe the light hurts its eyes."

The falcon flew to the plate glass where it bumped again and fluttered down to the broad sill. Gil was certain it was looking at him.

Julia turned off the light. "I think I'll go upstairs and sit in the jacuzzi," she said. "Do you mind?"

"Of course not."

"Do you have to get up early?"

Gil nodded. "I have a meeting with Cullen first thing in the morning."

"You didn't tell me."

"You didn't ask."

"What's he going to say?"

"He'll tell me whether my renderings are good or not good. He'll say yes or no."

"And you're not worried?"

"It's out of my hands."

The moon through the plate glass made muted shadows against the wall. The furniture was dark shapes—the sofa, the wingback chair, the coffee table, all black shapes. The chandelier glinted in the moving air. Through the living room, the dining-room table shone with a pale, flat light. The bird flew again, circling through the darkness. It came back again to the plate-glass window.

"Maybe you could get it to fly out through the sliding door in the kitchen," Julia said.

"I'll figure something out," Gil said.

Julia went to the stairs. "Will you wake me?" she asked. "I have to be at the stables at seven. "

He nodded, and Julia climbed the stairs. Her steps faded, and the diminishing sound made him conscious of her absence. She moved down the long hallway to the bedroom at the back of the house.

Gil had been educated in New Jersey, had started law school at Columbia, but dropped out because he hated it. For two years he worked as a draftsman for an architecture firm in the city and had lived with a French woman, Terèse, whom he met on the sidewalk at 103rd Street when she asked him directions. She had barely spoken English, and in the beginning, he sensed more than knew her interest in him was as a teacher of the language. They went to museums—the Met, the MOMA, the Frick—and took long walks. They were limited in what they could talk about, but she was lyrical with her body, a dancer in bed. He had loved her in a casual way, neither promising nor resisting.

Then her father made her return to Paris to finish her studies. When she was gone, he had fallen back into his work, not only drafting, but sketching trees, the pond in Central Park, people on the benches. Terèse wrote him a letter asking in her broken words what his intentions were, and he was surprised by what he took to be desperation. He loved her, but couldn't bring himself to answer. He knew she'd have learned English; they'd have conversed. But he was afraid of the immense part of her hidden in another language.

His mother died that fall, and he'd gone to North Carolina for her funeral and stayed the winter. He applied to architecture school, was accepted at MIT, and worked long hours at night, drifted through the days. He'd met Julia in a cafe. She had asked him the time.

All that was twelve years ago now, eleven married, eleven years of no great achievement, no particular future. Their house, which Julia had inherited from her father, was more than adequate. Because of her health problems, real or imagined, they had never had children. Gil was an associate in his firm, though from lack of ambition or vision, he had not advanced. He was on an island, unable to wave down a passing ship, and all he had to hope for was in the next hour or the next day another ship appeared on the horizon.

He walked through the adjoining dining room and the swinging door into the kitchen where he turned on the overhead light. The kitchen and den had been newly remodeled, and the glare from the immaculate counters and white walls hurt his eyes. A glass-topped table sat in a bay window overlooking the terrace. The sliding-glass door to the terrace was the largest opening in the house, but he did not see how the bird would get to the kitchen unless it wanted to.

He got down a glass, clinked in ice from the refrigerator door, and poured gin into it. On impulse, before he took a drink, he picked up the telephone and dialed the Eversons' number.

"Listen, Tom, it's Gil. I know it's late, but is Marie there?"

Tom didn't say anything, but Gil heard him call to Marie in the background. "It's Gil," Tom said. "Do you want to talk to him?"

There was a pause, and Marie came on.

"I want to apologize," Gil said.

"Well, you should," Marie said. "Did Julia put you up to this?"

"Not at all. She's in the jacuzzi. "

"Then I accept your apology."

"I have a couple of questions for you. There's a bird flying around my living room—a falcon, I think—not very big, with

a gray back and an orange tail. Do you know what it might be?
We think it came down the chimney."

"Kestrel," Marie said. "It used to be called sparrow hawk."

"Black markings on the face?"

"Yes."

"Thank you, Marie"

"You're welcome."

"Now can you tell me honestly George Bush didn't know
about Iran-Contra?"

Marie hung up the phone—slammed it down, Gil thought—
and he stood for a moment with the receiver in his hand, smiling.
Then he pulled open the sliding-glass door.

The light from the kitchen illuminated the flagstones and the
black-iron table and chairs and reached to the hedge. Then the
lawn sloped away toward the field. Gil stepped outside, felt the
cooler air of night time. The insects had quieted, and traffic had
ebbed, or perhaps the breeze through the dead leaves was louder
where he was. He walked out in front of the living room. The
kestrel was perched on the ledge of the plate-glass window, and
Gil felt keenly the bird's vision—the pale glow of the moon gave
the field an eerie radiance. It beckoned, as if home were close
and reachable, the night sky opening outward.

He set his gin on the coffee table in the living room and
approached the bird from behind the standing lamp. "Fly that
way," he said. He held his arms out horizontally as if to make
himself larger, took two more steps, and knocked into the lamp.
The lamp fell sideways and crashed into the end table. The bird
flew from the window and veered into the dining room.

Gil righted the lamp and edged around the sofa. The bird had
perched on the back of one of the oak chairs at the dining-room
table.

Gil paused in the wide doorway. "If I'd known you were
coming," he said, "I'd have set you a feast."

The bird tilted its head, and the moonlight caught its black eye.

"To whom are you talking?" Julia called from the stairs.

Gil heard Julia descend the stairs partway, but he couldn't see her. "The kestrel," he said.

"What was that noise?"

"I was trying to get the bird into the kitchen."

She came into the foyer and turned on the light there. The light diffused into the dining room. Her slippers swished into the living room, but Gil didn't look around. The kestrel spread its orange tail and flew from the chair into the mullioned windows, then back into the living room, where it settled again on the window ledge in the lower-left corner.

"Are you still drinking?" Julia asked. She picked up his glass and smelled it.

He didn't answer.

"Forget the bird and come to bed. I can't sleep with you down here knocking things over."

"You could help me."

"I'm not dressed."

He gazed at her. She stood with her back to the light in the foyer, draped in a blue towel. Her hair was loose and wet from the jacuzzi, and her skin looked soft, damp, clean of makeup. She looked beautiful, he thought, almost innocent.

"What are you doing?" she asked.

"Looking at you."

"Well, don't."

But he walked across the wood floor toward her. Her eyes held his. He did not know what she saw exactly—who knew what anyone else saw?—but she had to see him, his body moving toward her. Slowly. Each step closer he risked her turning away. But she didn't. He stopped in front of her, reached out his hand, and took hold of the edge of the towel.

She took a half-step backwards, but he didn't let go of the towel, and it gave way from her body. She pulled the towel back and covered herself again. Her eyes were shadows, but he didn't turn from her.

She didn't move or answer.

He stepped out of his shoes and peeled off each of his socks. He unbuttoned his shirt. He didn't know why she stayed where she was, but she watched him take off his white shirt, unzip his slacks, which slid down his hips to the floor. He stood before her in his underwear, his penis hard against the thin cotton.

"Do it," he said.

Her lower lip trembled, and a look came into her face. In the dim light he couldn't see her face clearly, but she lowered her eyes, not in shame or revulsion, but to look at him. He felt an eerie relief. Her eyes traveled down his bare chest, his unmuscled stomach, his erection, his thin legs, and back up. When her gaze reached his again, a sadness was in her eyes that made him shudder. It was he who turned away.

He woke in the darkness to cold, moving air. He shivered and pushed away the blanket he'd slept under, stood up from the sofa, stretched. The house was silent. A breeze ran from the kitchen through the dining room and out the open windows in the corner of the living room. He found his slacks and pulled them on, picked up his shirt from the floor and slid his arms into the sleeves. He listened, but there was no sound. Only the air moved.

He turned on the lamp on the end table. His glass of gin with the ice melted was untouched on the coffee table beside *The Art of the Prado*. The kestrel was on the floor beneath the plate-glass window. He picked it up and felt the loose bones in its neck, spread its patterned orange tail, tipped open the closed eyelid. He laid the bird gently on the windowsill and looked out the window. A pale light seeped from the east over the field and colors emerged in the apple trees and in the woods beyond.

Gregory Spatz

*Me at age three or so, just after I finally started to speak. Looking
at this picture I think I remember why I waited so long.
I was happy. I didn't feel like saying anything.*

Gregory Spatz grew up in the Berkshires, in Massachusetts, and was educated
at Haverford College, the University of New Hampshire, and the University
of Iowa Writers' Workshop. He is the author of a novel, *No One But Us*
(Algonquin). His short stories have appeared in *The New England Review, The
New Yorker, Shenandoah, The Indiana Review,* and elsewhere, and have received
honorable mention in the 1993 *Best American Short Stories* and in the Pushcart
Prizes, 1993. This year he is the recipient of a Michener grant. Prior to
becoming a full-time writer, Spatz earned his living as a bluegrass musician on
the West Coast. He lives with his two cats in Iowa City.

GREGORY SPATZ
Stone Fish

*O*ne day when I was thirteen my father and I were stacking wood in the shed behind our house. He had on a black-and-white wool plaid jacket he'd worn for years—one my mother had given him and which her father had worn as a young man. The collar and elbows were shaggy with burst threads. I'd been talking so much I could hardly stand the sound of my voice. Often when I was with him I'd get like that, talking to fill in the silence until the things I said were ridiculous and childish sounding. I was in love with a girl then because of her eyes. More than anything I wanted her to ride her bicycle past our house when I was outside with my shirt off, splitting wood. But we lived miles from the rest of the world, on a dirt road where the only cars that passed were neighbors' cars and friends of neighbors. It would take a long time being lost on a bicycle for anyone to wind up out here.

Talking to him I lost track of what I'd said and what I hadn't. I couldn't remember if I'd told him about her eyes, or having my shirt off when she rode by on her bicycle, or only about trying to work up the courage to ask her to the Ice Capades. I hated myself for having said this much, though at the same time I knew if I were to stop talking I would only feel in the silence as if he were reading my mind.

Glimmer Train Stories, Issue 23, Summer 1997
©1997 Gregory Spatz

"Jeremy," he said, finally, in an exasperated tone like he'd held out as long as he could not speaking. "Why fixate on her appearance? For God's sake, you don't even know her. Girls aren't just what they *look* like."

I knew this was essentially true, though I also knew it was the sort of truth no one paid attention to, including him. My mother was a beautiful woman. I still remembered the way she would lift me to her when I was small—her wide, crooked eyes and the widow's peak in her hair that was so sharp it looked carved. Before she left, she'd stood in front of me, squeezing her hands together like she wanted to keep something in them from escaping. I was about five years old. "You have a wonderful father," she said. "Never forget that. He'll take care of you and some day, when you feel like it, you can find me, wherever I am, and we'll go on just like before. What do you say?" I knew I shouldn't cry or cling or do any of the things she wasn't doing. "Yes," I said, and let her lift me to her one last time to kiss me before she left.

My father said, "You'll be unhappy for a very long time if you think I'm wrong about that."

We went on stacking wood. The calming logic of it, finding spaces and filling them with pieces of wood lain horizontally, made what we said seem unimportant—like we were only trying our ideas and didn't mean them. What really mattered was the wood. Still, I wished my mother were there. I wished she were inside like mothers on TV shows, and the mothers of my friends, heating up soup and getting ready to say things when we walked in the door, like, "You two must be freezing," or, "Here are my men!" Instead there would be the usual. My father would stir-fry chicken or tofu in the wok. Then he'd head off to the basement, to his workbench where he spent his evenings carving fish from blocks of marble and wood. I'd sit in my room reading ski magazines and bad novels until I was too bored to keep reading; then I'd go downstairs, sit on the couch, and play chords on his guitar, or deal myself a hand of solitaire.

A few years after she left I was sick for weeks with mumps and a high fever that made me hallucinate. My hallucinations were all in my ears and fingertips. I'd hear things louder than they were—my hair on the pillow crackling like a forest fire, my father yelling and stamping when in fact he was being his quietest. And without warning the feeling in my fingertips would become reversed and exaggerated so I couldn't feel the thing I was touching, only the pressure of my bones inside my skin and the prickly weight of my blood circulating.

One night my fever went over 105. He said I woke him up crying and talking. Nothing I said made sense. I don't remember that. I do remember lying on the bath mat at his feet, naked and unbelievably cold, his face distorted above me. I was on my stomach and could only see him from the corners of my eyes. He had a yellow enema bag in one hand and I was vaguely aware of a pressure building against the inner walls of my abdomen, also something icy trickling between my legs. "Be calm," he said and put one foot lightly on the small of my back to keep me still. "I'm right here," he said. I could feel the tiles under my cheek through the bath mat, and when I spread my arms I could feel them with my fingers—smooth, even grids of acrylic. I kept pressing and pressing in order to remember what real sensation felt like in case the finger hallucinations started.

Minutes later he sat me on the toilet and after that plunged me in freezing water, in the tub. "Be calm," he kept saying. "This is what we have to do." Later he told me it was a cure he'd learned from a book of holistic medicine my mother had left us. He shook out the thermometer and tried to stick it in my mouth, but I wouldn't let him. "Come on, Jeremy, cooperate. If we don't get this under control I'll have to take you to the hospital. Is that what you want?" My skin felt like it would break and my heart was choking me. I felt his hands on my shoulders, holding me down, and smelled water everywhere, heard my feet kicking in and out of it. "Please," I was yelling. He told me this later. "Please, please!" He said I was in the water for just about five minutes before he gave up. He dried me, carried me back to bed, and sat next to me the rest of the night, swabbing my back with alcohol until the fever broke.

When I woke up I had no real recollection of this. Only vaguely I remembered the enema and the cold water. He was still next to me in the chair, a look on his face that was both stern and frightened. I smelled rubbing alcohol and sweat soaked into my sheets, and I knew then I had almost died, but I didn't know what had stopped me. I was too warm and wasted to think about it. The humidifier behind him chugged out a thin stream of fog. He leaned forward and the chair creaked. It was a kitchen chair he had brought up weeks ago in order to sit next to me reading books aloud and playing card games. On the floor at his feet were my sick-things—games and sketchbooks, pill bottles, crumpled pjs, a teacup, Kleenex.

"How old are you?" he asked. His voice was steady.

"Eight," I answered.

"What's your name?"

"Jemmy," I said. It was my childhood name, the one he still called me by occasionally, though more and more, and always at school, I was Jeremy.

He breathed deeply in and out and rubbed his fingertips under his eyes. Then he asked me a few more simple questions—the president of the United States, how many quarters in a dollar, the name of the high school where he taught math. He got into the bed with me and held my head to his chest and said, "Okay. You're okay." I knew I should feel close to him, but I didn't. I wondered why, in all the years that had passed, we'd never touched like this.

For days afterward, even after the hallucinations stopped, I went on pretending there were things in my ears and under my fingertips he couldn't know about, just so he'd remember what it had been like to believe he was losing me. And later, when I was fully recovered and back in school, if I tried to bring up the night I'd almost died he'd shake his head or look sideways at me and raise one eyebrow, and say, "Died? I don't think so, Jem. You were pretty sick."

When the snow came, I kept track of it. If it came after dark I'd turn on the porch light outside and watch it swirl through the skirt of yellow light. The best snow in my opinion was a fast, heavy snow of small flakes. I could watch for hours, the way it whipped down, quick as static, always telling the same stories. The smaller the flakes the longer the snow was likely to last. Fat, plummy flakes, though dazzling, meant clearing skies and no accumulation—they represented a false hope since I wanted snow so thick it wiped out the world. If a snowfall came during the day and I wasn't at school, I'd stand at the kitchen window and measure it according to how well I could make out the trees on the far side of the neighbor's field. Best of all were mornings after a snowfall I hadn't known about—how the light would have lifted and brightened, making everything inside appear to me like I was seeing it for the first time.

The winter I turned fourteen the snow didn't come until February. There were squalls and flurries and storms that lasted an evening before blowing off or turning to rain, but no accumulation. I thought the ground looked tired and disgraced from being exposed all this time. My father never shared my interest in snow and I was trying hard then to seem more like him—quiet and stand-offish, with slight, practical answers ready for any question he might ask. I kept my disappointment to myself. After school I'd walk a mile or so into the woods along old tractor paths, to an abandoned Boys Club camp where there was a quarry, a watch tower, and a locked, decrepit bunk. I carried my skates around my neck, the laces knotted together, and a sandwich in my coat pocket for later. The skates banged each other every few steps and the laces cut at the back of my neck, so I'd have a sore feeling in my shoulders by the time I arrived, like I'd been staring for too long in one direction.

At the edge of the ice I'd stand a few seconds, appreciating the look of things, letting my feet settle against the cold insoles of my skates and feeling the heat trapped in the layers of my clothes continually seeping out and renewing itself. From where I was you couldn't really see the quarry or anything of the abandoned Boys Club. Too many trees were in the way. Dead cattails and dry, yellow humps of grass came up through the ice, and tree branches hung down at face level, like any swamp. But as you pushed out further the swamp gave way to frozen water stretching hundreds of feet in all directions. Sometimes at the end of an afternoon skating I'd have a hard time finding the inlet where my boots were and the trail home again. I'd circle around watching stars come out—past the rocky beach where the boys used to swim, and around the bend to the watchtower and the pine trees covering the upward slope to the top of Mt. Pisqua, and further out to a point that always made my heart race, where the ice and boulders ran into each other along the shore, and back again to another slope of pines stretching up.

One day there was a woman on a log next to the beach where the boys would have swum. She was in a bright purple coat, sitting forward with her hands on her knees. I stopped in the middle of the ice, dizzy for a second because I wasn't moving anymore. The flatness of ice in contrast with the surrounding hills made the land seem to swell up subtly. There was a boom like a gunshot from the other side of the quarry, some pressure far under the ice releasing, and then silence. I saw my skate tracks scratched all over the surface of the ice, wavering lines interrupted here and there by the patches of frost-barbed ice that were impossible to skate across, and trapped oxygen bubbles where my skate blades crumbled the surface. In a few months all those tracks would be gone and if I were standing here then I would be dead. Another reason for my dizziness.

"Hey," I yelled. I raised one arm and let it fall back at my side. She didn't move or acknowledge me. From where I was I couldn't even tell if she was looking in my direction. The wind went through the trees. Something—an empty plastic grocery bag, it looked like—blew past her, skittering and ballooning over the ice. Still she didn't move. I started wondering if I had yelled at all. In my mind I could go back to the seconds just before it and everything then was exactly the same as now. If I wanted to, I could pretend I hadn't seen her. I could skate once around the quarry until I came to where she was and pretend I was discovering her; then she might not feel strange about how I was staring from a distance and shouting.

I went the long way around, past the watchtower and the slopes of pine trees going to the top of Mt. Pisqua. Now and then I'd glance up to be sure she was still there, the ends of her coat moving in the wind, her face pointed away from me. The last time I looked she was finally watching me. I thought she was pretty in a familiar way, all her features going together like a doll's face. Her eyebrows were thick and dark, almost joining over the bridge of her nose.

I stopped in front of her. "I saw you across the water," I said. It seemed pointless now pretending I hadn't. I stood on the toes of my skates. I was out of breath. She smiled but said nothing, the edges of her smile compressing skin all the way back to her ears and wrinkling it fantastically. There were no buttons on her coat and she had a long, dirty, white scarf. I couldn't tell if she was Indian or Spanish. Her eyes were brown and green, like looking at the ground through ferns. Miranda, the girl I'd been in love with most of that year, had sapphire eyes that were so pretty I wanted to lick them. To me they were *things*, not eyes. This woman's eyes were not like that. "How come you didn't answer?"

"Did I have to?" Her voice was deep without being strained, almost delicate.

I thought back to the specific seconds when I was standing in the middle of the water. "I guess not."

"I came out here yesterday too. I saw you then." She looked at my feet. "Those are some nice skates. Are they your sister's?"

"Mother's," I said. "Just because they're white doesn't mean they're a girl's. Skates are all the same." These were my father's words coming through me.

"Yes, I see," she said. "I think they're fine. And does your mother know you're out here by yourself?" Before I could answer she went right on, "Of course. You don't look ill cared for." She smiled again. "What's your name?"

"Jeremy. "

"Mine's Lucy Sanders." She cleared her throat. "Can you do something for me now, Jeremy?"

"What's that."

She stretched her legs out straight in front of her and shut her eyes a second before going on. Her gloves were two different colors, one green, one tan, both of them ragged at the fingertips so I could see skin underneath and the smooth edges of her nails. "Skate one more time around the ice for me? I love to watch. It looks so freeing."

"Sure." I pushed off with one foot and squiggled back a few yards from her.

"I never could do that," she said.

"It's easy."

She blinked at me and fake-smiled, so I thought for a moment I must have said something to offend her. "How thick do you think the ice is?"

"Only a few feet, ten at the most," I said. "The water's over a mile deep—no one knows, really. A man drowned here a few years ago and they never found him. Scary, isn't it?"

"Not to me," she said.

I skated away from her full speed, heading back the way I'd come, crouched forward and swinging my arms. I dug as hard as I could with my toes and the edges of my skates, keeping my head up straight so I wouldn't lose balance. As I came out of my second turn and started heading for the trees, I looked over my shoulder to get a glimpse of Lucy watching me, but the shore was a blur and my eyes were tearing. I couldn't pick her out. Not until I finished my final turn and started heading back toward the Boys Club did I realize she was gone. I straightened up and stopped skating then, let the wind push me and listened to the sound my skates made on the ice. "Hey!" I yelled. I tried to imagine possible paths she'd taken, following them with my eyes, up from the log across the clearing to the rotten bunk, and past that into the woods. Next to the bunk was an old foundation with most of a chimney left standing from a house that had burned down years ago. Her purple coat should have been easy enough to spot even at this distance, but she was nowhere.

I spent the rest of that afternoon circling the quarry, feeling watched and alone. The ice continued to boom and snap every so often, startling me so much sometimes I felt my muscles tense and both skates lift off. A few times I thought I sensed her behind me on the shoreline somewhere. I'd stop and turn suddenly to see if she was there. Always, the shore was blank—no one, just the bare trees and dead leaves and sticks covering the ground, some patches of ice and rocks showing through silver and white. When the sun started going down and the sky over the hills turned the same brown as the ground, only luminous, I found my boots and jacket and skated with them to the other side of the quarry where I had last seen her. I sat on the log where she'd been sitting and ate half the sandwich while I untied my skates, the other half while I slid into my boots. Some swirly, dense clouds at the top of Mt. Pisqua caught the last light of the sun, making it look like the mountain was on fire. The wind had died down by now and the woods were almost utterly silent.

I inhaled until my lungs were tight and shouted, "Lucy Sanders! I'm going home! If you're here, you should probably come with me or you'll freeze to death!" My voice faded off and echoed at the other side of the quarry. I heard a stick snap somewhere to my right and looked quickly, but there was nothing. Again, it was silent. "Okay," I said. I pulled my jacket around me and zipped up, left my skates on the ice next to the log, and headed across the clearing to the bunk. My arms in the jacket made a quiet hissing noise against my sides. As I walked, I kept looking left and right but nothing moved anywhere in the woods. The bunk was locked as always, with nothing new inside—the same shadows and carved graffiti, bottles, broken windows, and bits of glass on the floor. Everywhere I looked things were undisturbed. I went back across the clearing to the foundation, took a few steps into the bushes behind the old chimney, and kicked over some milk bottles and half a ruined dresser drawer left from the fire, its plastic liner fluttering in the breeze. I cupped my hands around my mouth. "Lucy!" I called. I waited a few more seconds and when nothing happened I headed down to the ice, picked up my skates, and went back across the quarry just as the stars were coming out.

At home I found my father in the basement under the floodlights dabbing black paint around the eyes of an elegant, two-foot-long balsa salmon and touching up the outlines of his gills and scales. Another fish he was working on, only half exhumed from a chunk of marble, lay next to him on the carving block surrounded by his different-sized chisels. I loved watching him carve—his hammer taps at the back of a chisel making its point slip and jump over the form of a fish, back and forth, up and down, hacking away bits of stone or wood to find the fish's shape. He always seemed happiest to me then. He'd stand on the balls of his feet and arch his back and move around the block of stone patiently, like he was slow dancing.

"Hey, Jeremy," he said. "I was just starting to wonder where you were." He looked at me a moment, maybe waiting for me to say something about skating. "Hungry?" he asked.

"Not really yet." The smell of his oil paint came across the room at me. He had on his old plaid wool jacket and a denim work apron underneath, covering most of his thighs. Behind him the space heater suddenly came on, lit up, and started rattling, turning the floor around him orange.

"How's school?"

Always the same questions. Behind them he wanted more, I just didn't know what. Sometimes it seemed he could as easily have poked me in the chest to see if I had a response as ask these redundant questions. "Okay, I guess. Boring."

He stood up straight and looked at me a second, screwing the cap back on the tube of black paint. Then he went to the sink to rinse his brush. I knew he was trying to think of other things to ask me now—a test he'd known I was preparing for, a paper, a girl, a teacher whose anecdotes were worth repeating. He had been late after school for a staff meeting that day and we hadn't seen each other since morning. "Let's go up," he said. "I'm hungry even if you aren't." He pulled the plug on the floodlights and heater, unknotted his work apron, slid it from around his neck, and draped it over the half-made stone fish.

I indicated with my chin. "He's looking good," I said.

"It's a she. Maybe two of them. I can't tell yet." I knew if I looked more closely I'd see his faint pencil marks scratched around the sides of the stone—meaningless, indecipherable notes to himself about where the fish might lie in the stone.

"Who's it for?"

He passed me and headed up the stairs. "No one. I thought it'd look nice on the front porch, maybe." Our feet shuffled over the grit and made the bare plank stairs ring. "Or maybe I'll give it to your grandparents for their anniversary in May." He laughed. "Should be done by then. Wipe your feet," he said and waited to let me pass before switching off the lights and closing the basement door. I don't know when, exactly, but sometime between seeing him down there outlining the details on his salmon and arriving back at the top of the stairs, I had decided not to tell him about Lucy. I saw my skates lying together on their sides on the mat next to the front door and heard her voice in my head and I knew I wouldn't say anything.

"Hey," he said, as I stepped around him. "You have good color today." He put his hand on my cheek.

"It's the wind."

After dinner I sat at the kitchen table and he coached me through math problems, gently scolding me for having so little interest in his subject. The sour smell of his breath and his heat coming through the back of my shirt as he leaned over me, vigorously scratching out numbers and theorems in pencil, left-handed, kept waking me up and putting me to sleep. "See how this changes the fraction, so the unknown, x, comes out on the top, and then you can use your law of inequality to simplify it further ..." Always, things worked out for him in this rational, speechless, pencil landscape. I hated it. I pictured us like dogs, me chasing after him while he went around barking and digging up piles of leaves to show me where the secret numbers were and how to locate them later on without him. At the end I wrung my forehead in my hands. "Okay, okay, I understand, I just don't get how you did it. Now can I go to bed?"

Q.E.D., he printed at the bottom of the page, and laughed. "See you in the morning."

The next day was warm and overcast. After school I walked across the fields separating the middle school from the senior high where my father taught. Cross-country skiers in tights and wool hats were running the periphery of the school grounds, leaping and stabbing their poles in the dirt to simulate skiing, and hooting to each other. "It's gonna snow!" one of them would yell, and the other team members would yell back, "Yeah! Snow! Snow! Snow!" They had been doing this since November, trying to encourage the sky to let loose. "Snow!" one yelled. "Tomorrow!" They seemed more desperate than ever. Their hats, all bright blues, pinks, purples, and blacks with stripes and zigzag patterns, no two the same, stood out sharply against the yellow-brown ground and gray trees. I watched them huff around the side of the middle school and disappear, their cheering voices following like a wake. It wouldn't snow. Already the air was wet and smelled sweet like cold rain.

My father was in the math office waiting for me, clipping his fingernails. He had pudgy, muscular fingers. When I was younger he kept the fingernails on his right hand as long as a woman's to play the guitar, but he rarely played now, and when he did he used a flat pick. He looked up when I came in the door, lowered his feet from his desk, and sat forward so his desk chair creaked. There were three books in the steel shelves over his desk—a dictionary and two math texts—and a withered aloe plant, more brown than green, with crumbs of dirt around it. One other teacher was in the room, a little man with gray-blond hair, scoring tests with a red pencil. "See you," my father said. "See you, Phil," the man said, not looking up, and we left.

Walking out of the school we barely spoke. Once, leaving his office alone at this hour, I had come around a corner and almost bumped into two lovers, both of them with long, curly, blond hair, standing against the wall with their mouths stuck together and their shirts untucked. I had hurried by and once I'd gotten a safe distance, stopped to watch a while, to see if they ever got tired or changed position. Their hands slipped in and out of each other's clothes. The boy rocked against the girl, making the locker behind her clang. Then the girl was suddenly looking right at me over the boy's shoulder. She had black eyebrows and eyelashes in spite of her blond hair. "Take a picture, it lasts longer," she said. Now, every time I walked by the spot where the lovers had been, I thought of them like they were still there. I remembered the insulting, half-provocative tone of her voice and felt the same numbness, not knowing what in the world to say back to her. I tried to imagine an expression on my face that was as close to the tone of her voice as possible. Still I didn't know what I'd say to her.

"So, what's new with you?" my father asked.

"Nothing *new*," I said. "What do you think?" For a second I wondered if my thoughts about the lovers had somehow slipped up and shown themselves without my realizing it. I glanced at him and watched the way his head bobbed forward and back when he walked. We were almost the same height then. I had his hair—black and straight with a part on the side, although his was longer and mixed with silver in front. He looked back at me and smiled tightly, two patches of puffy dry skin at either end of his mouth lifting so his smile looked bracketed.

"Just asking," he said. He dropped his smile so the dry patches extended downward from the corners of his mouth again, giving him an exaggerated fish-frown.

Outside it smelled even more like rain. This was too depressing to think about—more rain, no snow. I ran ahead of him and circled his old Impala, chanting, "Snow, snow, snow," until he caught up with me. He had his keys out, ready to unlock the door. I almost knocked into him, but he stepped aside at the last second.

"What the hell's the matter with you?" he asked.

"What's the matter with *you*?" I retorted, and circled the car again, banging on the roof and fenders with my fist while he revved the engine.

"Come skating with me when we get home," I said, slinging my knapsack next to his, on the seat between us. "May be our last chance for a while. If it rains." I didn't know why I was asking him this. All day I had looked forward to getting out there alone, seeing if I could find Lucy, tracking her as completely as possible for as long as there was light. I didn't want him along. I wanted him to know there was something hidden and not to know what it was or that I was deliberately hiding it.

"Don't think so, Jem. I have about a hundred tests to grade

tonight." He put his arm across the seat and looked over his shoulder, backing out of the parking space. "And unless I'm mistaken you have a few other things to take care of yourself." As we drove out of the lot he began listing chores I'd neglected all week in order to skate—the wood, the laundry, the vacuuming, my bedroom.

"Okay, okay, give it a rest," I cut in. "I get the picture."

We drove in silence. Turning off the main highway onto the long dirt road home, he put his hand on my shoulder. A man who lived up the road passed us heading the other way, the hood and front grate of his pickup so skewed to one side it looked as if he was aiming to drive off the road. My father raised one finger on the steering wheel at him and the man raised his back. "You're a good kid," he said. "You know that?"

"No."

He patted me twice and withdrew his hand from my shoulder.

Coming around the last corner at the top of the ridge we could see our house for a moment below—bay green, with six windows in front and wide, white, window trim, the broad, peaked back of the roof almost hidden in trees. "Home sweet home!" he used to say, when I was younger, as we passed this point in the road. Now he said nothing. His face relaxed, his eyebrows leveling and stretching back and the corners of his mouth softening. And then we were going much faster. The gravel popped under us and rocks rang against the wheel-wells and the floor. Through the side window I saw more trees and gray sky, oaks and ashes trapped in the curved, dirty window glass.

That night it rained. I kept waking up and falling asleep again. Rain rattled in the gutters and blew down through the trees and spattered against the side of our house. Toward dawn I thought I heard a door slam downstairs and got up to see what it was. But nothing looked out of place—the doors and windows were all shut, lights off, and chairs standing empty. Outside was a faint

dawn glow, barely purple, coming through the trees. I flipped
on the porch light where I had always liked watching the snow
come down and saw the wet porch floorboards, gleaming and
bare. Then I went back upstairs and down the hall, into my
father's room, where it was peacefully dark still and smelled of
his sleep. He was on the floor on bamboo mats next to the
window where my mother's sewing machine had been, the
futon they had shared folded against a wall and covered with his
books and papers and opened letters and cassette tapes. I squatted
next to him and his eyes opened right away. "What time is it?"
he asked, his voice completely alert as if he hadn't been sleeping
at all.

"I don't know. About four. Four or five."

He yawned and stretched. "Can't you sleep?" he asked.

I shook my head. I wished I didn't care. I wished the rain
soaking through the ground outside and lighting up every
surface with its gleaming, watery outline didn't bother me. "It's
raining," I said.

"Yes," he said. "I know." He sighed and shut his eyes.

There was a gust of wind and I smelled rain mixed with a
smell of thawing earth coming through the crack in his window.
I felt it in the air touching my face and bare ankles and there
was nothing I could think of to console myself—no pleasing
harmony between what was and what should have been;
between what I imagined and what was true; between words
and the things they were. I didn't know why I felt this out of
joint, or how to say anything to him about it.

"Lie down," he said. "Nothing worse than being by yourself
when you can't sleep." He threw part of a blanket over me,
rolled onto his side facing me and said, "Wake me up if you want
to talk."

I lay there listening to his clock hum and the quiet sound of
his breaths in and out, trying not to think about the rain. For a
while I shut my eyes and imagined myself departing through

gray water as dim as the light seeping across the ceiling. But it was no good. I rolled onto my side and saw him next to me in his V-neck T-shirt, hands folded in front of his face, and his hair falling across the bridge of his nose and the crescent dent in his cheek where he'd fractured his cheekbone one night falling down stairs. More and more his skin was settling against the structure of his face, narrowing it, so I could see the shape of his bones and muscles inside. I wondered if he had looked this old for a long time and I hadn't noticed, or if his being asleep made him look older. He would be forty-eight that summer.

When his alarm went off he reached behind his pillow for it without opening his eyes. Seconds later he sat up, rubbing his face and stretching. "Sleep at all?" he asked. He put his hand on my leg a moment.

"Not really," I said. "Sort of."

He grunted. His knees clicked as he drew his feet up under himself, stood, and stepped over me to get to the bathroom. There were thin, burst veins in his calves like wire, and his feet were yellow and chafed, the nails on his big toes thick as shells. "You can tell me what's bothering you," he said, as he went across the room.

"Sure," I said.

He yawned. "Go get ready for school. We'll talk about it on the way." We wouldn't talk. I knew that. The bathroom door creaked open and shut and I heard the shower water come on, and suddenly I was unbelievably sleepy. I rolled into the spot where he had been, shut my eyes, and fell instantly to sleep

The next time I saw Lucy Sanders was Saturday, the weekend after it rained. She was at the colder, west side of the quarry in the shadow of the mountain, hunched between the big rocks on the shore as if she'd lost something. "Lucy," I shouted. I was still closer to the middle of the quarry.

She spun around to face me and after a second waved with

both arms. I waved back. "Come here! You have to see this!"

"What?"

She didn't answer.

I continued at the same speed I'd been going, stretching my legs behind me and feeling the sun on my face until I went under the shadow of the mountain, and for a few seconds I felt plunged in darkness. I blinked hard and waited for my eyes to clear. When they did I saw she was kneeling next to a rock, her purple coat splayed on the ice around her. Her face, in profile, was almost too squat to call pretty; then she turned toward me and I was taken by her eyes again, her eyebrows, and the shape of her mouth. "Come here," she repeated. "There are fossils!"

I stopped and carefully lowered myself onto my knees next to her. "What fossils?"

"Look," she said. She pointed at some faint traces in the surface of the rock before her. "See?" she asked.

I leaned closer. There were hair-fine white lines in the rock— quartz striations and a few black nubs that looked like ordinary bumps. "No," I said. "Where?"

"You have to look hard." She pointed again, her finger moving slowly over the jagged surface of the rock. "See? Trilobites—they look a little like sea-horses. Can you see it now?"

I couldn't, but to please her I pretended I did. "Ah ha," I said, and nodded a few times. I was hot from skating, but cold too, the sweat freezing all over me. Looking at the rock, my fingers suddenly began to feel numb and bloated. This still occasionally happened—a pattern in something I saw or heard would set me off and I would feel the mild beginnings of an hallucination. "Cool," I said. I rubbed my mittens up and down against my thighs.

"One of the first exoskeletal life-forms known. Paleozoic, I think." She leaned back on her knees and gestured to the many half-submerged rocks surrounding us. "I've been finding them all over this afternoon. It's amazing. Come on. I'll show you."

I got up and went after her, walking on the toes of my skates, occasionally gliding a step or two where there was enough open space between rocks. I pounded my hands together. "Is that what you're doing here?" I asked. She glanced back at me. "Looking for fossils or something?"

"I'm not doing anything. Why do I have to be *doing* anything?" She threw her arms out dramatically, let them drop at her sides, and laughed. I could see she enjoyed saying this, though I wasn't sure if she really meant it. Now she stopped next to another rock, put her hand out, and leaned close to it. She had a look on her face like she was getting ready to greet someone she hadn't seen in a long time. I imagined her breath frosting the rock surface. "Yup. This is another one," she said. "Oh! They're much more defined here. Come look."

I put my hand on her shoulder a moment to steady myself and leaned as close to the rock as she was. This time I was pretty sure I saw them—fossilized triangular bugs like kites, some rightside up, some upside down. I moved in closer and closer, but I was still worried about hallucinating. The wind blew up the back of my sweater. She was talking about prehistoric times and the formation of sedimentary rock, but I couldn't concentrate. "Oh, look at this!" She dropped to her knees, pointing. "Look, look! Doesn't it just take you out of yourself?"

"Yes," I said.

"And look at this!" she said, trailing her finger over the rock. "Ferns!"

"Cool," I said. I turned around to face the quarry. A flock of finches—hundreds of them, it looked like—going over the ice wheeled suddenly together and headed in the other direction, light turning yellow and white on their backs as they beat their wings, so they looked like a place where the air had turned solid and started churning. I looked down at Lucy again, her dirty hair sticking under her collar and going across her shoulders, and I wanted to put my hand on her head, or under her hair on her neck. At the same time I wanted to get as far from her as possible. "Hey," I said. "It's freezing. Aren't you freezing? Let's go back out into the sun."

She glanced at me and blinked, her expression slowly tightening like she couldn't figure out what I was saying, then she looked back at the rock and her face relaxed again. "Aren't they nice? They don't know a thing. They just sit here."

When she stood up I noticed a faintly sour smell about her, like bad butter. I disliked it, though as soon as it had shifted away from us in the breeze I wanted it back again. A few raised white dots stood out in the skin under her eyes and along her jaw—more signs of her being unclean. She stood hunched forward with her hands in her pockets to keep her coat closed.

"Want to come?" I asked.

She looked at me a second, then away, and shrugged. "No," she said. She lifted her hands, still inside her pockets, so her coat opened and I saw she had on a worn green cardigan buttoned up wrong. "Maybe next time," she said, and lowered her hands.

"What next time?"

"Next time I see you."

I frowned and shook my head to let her know I was perfectly aware there would be no next time.

She took a step forward so one of her feet was touching mine, and put her hand on my shoulder. "You look unhappy," she said. "Why so unhappy? At your age life should still be one good thing after the next." Up close she smelled more musty than sour and for the first time I realized I was a few inches taller. Then she pulled me to her and her mouth covered the side of my mouth and part of my cheek. I breathed in and tasted her strange smell at the back of my throat—an acid sweetness. I shut my eyes and gave myself over until there was only her cold skin and spit and the smell of her to let me know I was in the world. When she released me I didn't dare brush her saliva from the corner of my mouth, though it burned in the cold air. She stepped back from me and I watched her face receding, our eyes still fused, and for a second I was dizzy. "I'm responding to your need—your unhappiness and need. That's all," she said.

"But I'm not unhappy." I couldn't get my eyes out of hers. She scowled. I felt like a liar though I was pretty sure I was telling the truth. "I like my life."

She shook her head and started walking away. "Tell your mother to buy you some new skates so you can give me those. Girls' skates are for girls, anyway."

"Wait!" She was on the ground now, walking quickly away. I went right to the edge of the water.

"No! Don't follow," she said. "I'll see you again sometime." She continued up into the woods and in a few minutes I couldn't see her at all. I still heard her snapping sticks and breaking through underbrush every few minutes. Soon there wasn't even that. I turned back to the quarry and that flock of finches dropped down and broke open at the heart of the water, heading in two directions and then weaving back together. They went right above me, and the sound of their wings beating, a familiar rushing noise, was gone in the same instant it became audible.

By the end of the day I had lost interest in skating. I could skate forward and backward. I could cross over my left skate when I was going into a turn full speed. But I couldn't leap or spin or pirouette. Worse than that, I didn't care. I was tired of the wind on my face, and the mountain, and the trees, and the Boys Club repeating themselves over and over as I circled the quarry. Now the sky was filling with clouds. When I looked up suddenly sometimes I would remember the exact feel of Lucy's lips touching the side of my mouth, and the cold, star-shaped mark she had left on my skin. Then, as suddenly as I had remembered, I would forget. There was a sickle moon, bright in the pale sky between the clouds. I felt pierced through when I looked up and saw it and remembered her kissing me; already I couldn't tell what I remembered and what I was making up.

Later that winter my father finished his sculpture of the two stone fish. They were fat, spawning she-fish fighting upstream with their tails half-entwined in the same bit of rough, unfinished stone. I was with him when he was finishing their heads and faces, tapping around them with a flat chisel for smooth surfaces, then the sharpest one for outlines. He kept stepping back and cocking his head to one side, then moving in quickly to change some little detail. "Pop, tell me a story," I said. I didn't care what he said as long as he spoke so I wasn't left alone, tempted to fill in the silence, and then judging myself badly for what I said.

He kept on tapping, going around the fish, sending up a spray of stone, finding more and more detail for their faces. "What story?" he said.

"I don't know. Anything at all."

He hit a little harder, his strikes coming three at a time, a bright metal-on-metal sound—tink tink *tink*, tink tink *tink*, tink tink *tink* tink—with lower, bass undertones from the stone absorbing the shock. "When we lived in Italy, your mother and I, before you were born, we used to go out in a rowboat every day. Almost every day." His voice tightened as he leaned to one side to see something. "We were living in a hostel and didn't have much privacy otherwise." He stood straight, rubbed one fish's cheek with his thumb and then tapped twice, lightly, with the sharp chisel to make a crease in it. "She used to say that to me."

"Say what?"

"Tell me," he went to the other side of the fish to do its opposite cheek the same way, "a story."

"I'm bugging you, huh?"

"No."

"Then what stories did you tell her?"

Tink *tink*. "I don't remember."

"You do so."

He sighed. "She liked pretending we were that couple in the movie where the young soldier rows to Switzerland with his girlfriend all night to escape the German army. I forget what it was called. She liked stories like that. People on the run. We were in Italy ourselves to avoid the draft—for me to avoid the draft, so I guess it was a parallel situation, though times were very, very different." He rubbed one fish's mouth a few times with his little finger and shook his head, then went over it again, tapping lightly. I pictured him in a white T-shirt while a woman who looked like me taunted him, leaning forward in a rowboat and asking for stories. Switzerland, I reminded myself, and added steep, white-capped mountains behind them with gondolas and skiers and mountaineers. Then I became distracted thinking about this and lost the picture of the couple in the boat.

"Tell me more," I said.

"Nothing to tell." He set down his chisels and stood back to look at the fish. "I think that's it," he said. He put both hands on the small of his back where he said he sometimes had a spasm of warm feelings, finishing one of his sculptures. "Yes, yes. I really think so. Do you think?"

"Looks good to me."

He unknotted his apron and went to the sink to wash his hands, still glancing over his shoulder at the fish every few seconds as if he thought he might catch them at something unexpected. They weren't really done. Tomorrow he would come down, see every last thing and really finish them. Then he'd tell me to come look again. He would be beaming, walking around on the balls of his feet, and he might say a few strange things about how life and light and form reiterate one another in stone.

"Pa, did you love her?"

He turned the spigots hard to stop the water and I heard pipes overhead clang from the change in pressure. He flicked his hands dry. The water in the basement was unfiltered, gold-amber with a red sediment you could see in the bottom of a jar if you left it overnight. I imagined the drops flying from his fingers, red liquid jewels splashing the cement wall and clinging to the spigot handles in front of him. "Of course I loved her," he said. "Why do you think we were married?" The way he said this I knew it wasn't why they'd married, though I was also pretty sure he loved her. He shook his head as he went by me, touched me lightly on the shoulder with two wet fingers and headed upstairs. "You coming?" he called from the top of the stairs.

"In a minute," I said. I wanted to be alone admiring his fish—how they curved in opposite directions like a pair of parentheses, one going high, the other low, both of their bellies half-sunk in the rock. They were not looking at each other, but from the way their heads angled I knew they wouldn't collide. They were the most real-looking fish I'd seen him make in a while, and for the first time I was noticing how much they resembled him—the dented cheek and the frown that wasn't a frown. I rubbed my finger in the groove between them to feel the unfinished stone, and tried to imagine how in the world he knew what was fish and what was rock when he was carving. There was a song in my head then, one he used to sing about a pony and a girl. I hadn't heard him sing it for years. I remembered sitting in the tub as a small child, hearing them downstairs singing, their voices like the stone fish going one over the other, high and low, slipping around each other and not colliding. Tree limbs blew back and forth in the skylight above me in the tub and I felt warm and protected, though I also felt like I didn't exist. I was skylight, the tiled floor, steamy walls, and the sound of their voices.

Upstairs he was in the kitchen heating beans in the frying pan. They smelled good, sizzling as he spun them around in the butter with a metal spoon. I came up behind him and leaned my head on his shoulder a second. He lowered his head so his ear pressed against me. "Want lunch?" he asked.

"No."

I sat at the table—watched him sprinkle in salsa, cayenne, and salt, then roll the beans in a flour tortilla with grated cabbage and cheese. He ate leaning against the stove, holding the tortilla in one hand and a plate under his chin with the other. Neither of us spoke, but I was pretty sure we were thinking the same thing: we were wondering what things would be like for us if she returned, maybe for the first time thinking of her not as someone who was absent but someone who was truly gone.

Mid March we were running low on wood. By then snow had piled waist high on either side of the road and was about two feet thick on the roof. The last two days had been gorgeous, fake-spring, close to sixty degrees, and I was outside in the brilliant sun, knocking apart pieces of fruit wood—half a cord my father had gotten for cheap from a man up the road. I wore a bandanna around my forehead and had my T-shirt hanging from my back pocket like a tail. Now and then I'd stop splitting and go look at my reflection in the car window—my muscles stretching and distorted in the tinted glass, my thick, crow black hair, and my ribs rippling in and out with my breaths. I had on a pair of his old ski glasses and when I leaned close to the window I could see a reflection of my reflection in them; closer still and I saw behind the glasses, my eyelids flipping up and down, the lashes and pink folds of my eyelids magnified.

Around noon I hit a section of trunk that was exceptionally easy, wood dividing like butter for me. I felt very powerful, bouncing up on the balls of my feet, running the maul right through, and tossing split pieces aside, enveloped in the ketchup-sweet smell of burst wood fibers. I kept imagining my mother coming up the road behind me in our old car, the white station wagon, pulling herself from behind the wheel and raising her sunglasses on her forehead, then standing with one arm over the top of the door, admiring me, staring, not really smiling, half-stricken by my new appearance to her. I could see this so clearly it made my heart race and my skin prickle with anticipation. I saw her brown-gray hair and green eyes—the one lazy one that made her look almost cross-eyed from certain angles. Her voice would be sweet and slow when she said my name. I saw it so clearly once or twice I had to stop and turn around to convince myself she wasn't there.

Soon my father came outside in his running shorts. He stood next to me a while watching, and didn't say anything. I knew he wanted to split some before his run but didn't realize it yet, or didn't want to interrupt my rhythm.

"Here," I said finally, dropping the maul and stepping around him. "You do a few. I'm whipped." I went to lean against the hot fender of his car to watch. He was much faster than I was and more efficient, completely focused on the wood. There were no dreamy pauses between one swing and the next. He was so fast he could hit a piece of wood that was wobbling out of balance— knock it in two pieces before it fell. Now and then he'd look up as he was throwing aside split pieces and our eyes would meet and there was a question in them I didn't understand. *What?* he seemed to be asking. *What is it?* Then before I could say anything or begin a conversation he was finding another piece of wood, moving more and more quickly, setting it up, whacking it in half.

"All yours," he said when he was done, and ran by me out to the road, one hand raised to slap mine as he passed. We were as separate and alike as his stone fish, sunk in the silence not because of my mother but because of all our likeness, and because, for now, there was nothing more to say.

Linsey Abrams

*Yours truly at eight, with my maternal grandfather, painting
his fence my grandmother's favorite color, turquoise blue. The most
famous product of the industrial-chemical company he owned was a
soap powder called Flash. This was also the name of his company.
Flash could remove even turquoise-blue paint from your
hands, and if you didn't watch it, your skin.*

Linsey Abrams is the author of three novels, *Our History in New York*, *Double
Vision*, and *Charting by the Stars*. Her short stories have been published in
several magazines, including the *New Directions* annual, *Redbook*, *Mademoiselle*,
Kalliope, *Seattle Review*, *Thirteenth Moon*, *Colorado Review*, *Central Park*, *Chris-
topher Street*, and *Bomb*. They have been anthologized in *Best Short Fiction*,
Bantam, 1986, and *Tasting Life Twice*, Avon, 1995. She has also written essays
on contemporary literature for *The Mississippi Review*, *Quimera* (Barcelona),
The Review of Contemporary Fiction, the anthology *Writers & Their Craft*, and for
broadcast on WNYC Radio. She was interviewed most recently for *Teaching
Literature*, Cork University Press.

Abrams is co-director of the graduate writing program at Sarah Lawrence
College and writer-in-residence in the masters program of the City College of
New York. She is the founding editor of *Global City Review*.

LINSEY ABRAMS
The Theory of General Relativity

*J*t was three years after Rodger's death, and by then, my father, one of Eisenhower's navigators in World War II, also had died. In this same time period, we had moved my mother, who in her youth had worn the Hope Diamond for an entire evening, reluctantly into senior housing. Helen continued to be my own fixed star, a different kind of jewel, in a heaven of predictably moving constellations. But as for me, I had been diagnosed with a kind of neurological disorder, a slippage of some internal clock that matched neither Eastern Standard nor Greenwich Mean Time, let alone the music of the spheres.

Who knew such things existed or that the universe inhabited our beings in such incredibly specific ways? I kept thinking of Einstein's General Theory of Relativity: where two observers moving at great speeds will disagree about measurements of length and time in respect to each other's system. Only, in this case, I was the odd woman out. Now I took an array of drugs and shone a 41K high-intensity lamp in my face for exactly thirteen minutes every morning, to ensure that my thoughts neither speeded up nor slowed down. I should probably add that there was a psychiatric term for this condition that I almost never used. Call me a recovering romantic.

Glimmer Train Stories, Issue 23, Summer 1997
© 1997 Linsey Abrams

Meanwhile, Victor was sick, the AIDS finally having hit him full force. Over the last few years, his ex-boyfriend Ed Moss had become an expert on his diagnoses and near-death experiences, of which there had been several. But after a seemingly endless string of opportunistic infections and even a bout with lymphoma, the disease had abated suddenly, due to a new medication he was taking. Or something else perhaps. Not that any of us presumed to know, any more than we knew why Rodger had died so quickly.

It was a morning in mid-August, and Victor and I were making plans over the phone to see a movie later, something we had once done so casually. But now that neuropathy had affected his feet and balance, that summer we chose to go on weekday afternoons when the crowds were most manageable. Helen would meet us for an early dinner in a restaurant after work, so that we'd be able to do all the things we'd once done, if in a different manner.

In our usual panoramic conversational style, Victor and I had already covered the question as to whether Sydney, my only truly significant ex, had sold her soul to the devil—something Victor insisted she had, but, being sentimental, I couldn't quite agree to. It was true she'd stopped returning my calls a few years before, but in a way I had trouble believing was calculated. On the other hand, that had been my downfall all along with Sydney, giving her the benefit of the doubt as I watched her dig a hole, suspiciously life-size, that later she'd push me into. Still, affairs of the heart didn't fall under the exact category Victor and I had been discussing.

Specifically, what had so outraged him was that though Sydney had deserted him, too, somewhere along the way ... now that he was sick, it meant something different. Seeing her featured on page six of the *New York Post*, hobnobbing with the rich and famous, drove him to distraction, though he'd hobnobbed within that same circle, himself, once upon a time. So it wasn't the social scene, or even the delusional self-importance of those people, that bothered Victor. It was that Sydney, upon entering it, had left her old friends behind.

"Doesn't it upset you," he asked, "that she no longer speaks to you? It upsets me that she no longer speaks to me."

"I have Helen," I said, which in my life meant something akin to having booked the Titanic, only to find your travel plans unexpectedly altered. "Plus my relationship with Sydney was so long ago, it might have been light years," I told him. But there was something I didn't say, because I hardly understood it myself. In spite of all the terrible goings-on I'd had with Sydney, I still loved her. And that had nothing to do with how well she loved me back or had then, or the fact that I loved Helen in a deeper, fuller way, or that Sydney would never be in my life again. Or maybe it had to do with all those things.

Abruptly, our conversation turned to the new *New Yorker*, which Victor was scanning for movie possibilities. But the listings were no longer presented geographically, catering to the regionalism Manhattanites so cherish, thus it was no longer user friendly. Meanwhile, I was getting nowhere with the *Times*.

"For two people who are experts at using the library, this is a pretty lame effort," Victor said.

"It's because we don't have the proper sources," I told him. "Wait, I'm going to get *New York* magazine, which Helen says she buys for the listings. I guess until now I never really believed her." I got up to look at the months' worth of magazines and catalogues by the chair Helen always sat in in the living room. In the newer, bigger apartment we lived in now, there was more room to stack things. Miraculously, I found it and returned to the couch.

"Is that the August 13th issue?" Victor asked.

"Yes," I said.

"Well, brace yourself for the picture of Sydney at a luncheon for Donna Karan."

"Another party," I commented, "for that fashion designer whose clothing looks like funeral attire. Don't those people ever go to work?"

"That is their work. They're celebrities," Victor said. "Now turn to page eighty-eight."

The only thing I could think as I leafed forward in the magazine, and found the picture, was that though Sydney, as photographer to the stars, frequently was the object of publicity herself, at least it had its limits. I had one friend, a working but never-famous actress, who always had to see her ex-husband on the tabloids in the supermarket checkout, where you're often close to suicide already.

"Victor, you're amazing, remembering the exact page, off the top of your head like that." Honestly, after what he'd gone through in the past few years, I was surprised he could concentrate on anything.

"All I do anymore is read magazines and the newspaper, or go to the movies sometimes," Victor answered. "Plus I have dinner with friends, in or out, depending on whether it's a good- or a bad-foot day." That's how he referred to his neuropathy. "So now I'm a sort of idiot savant in regard to page numbers."

"All right, where are the movie listings?" I tested him.

"Fifty-three," he said, and of course he was right.

Victor and I went only to gay movies now. I wasn't sure exactly how this had happened, since with someone else I would have trekked up to the Paris at 59th Street to see the re-release of *Belle de Jour* that afternoon. And so, no doubt, would he. But it wasn't part of our agreed-upon repertoire, which had to do, both of us knew, with Victor's PWA status, not to mention larger issues of how each of us thought about our identity and sexuality now. On the other hand, both Victor and I felt it necessary to research sensibilities that might not remind us of ourselves. We were looking for information, simply, now that it was available.

For our first movie, that summer, we'd seen the one about the gay priest in Ireland. At first he hates himself, nothing new for either a gay person or a Catholic, I thought at the time. But then there was a surprise, because a girl was being molested by her father, though, according to church doctrine, the priest, who still believed in his vows at that point, couldn't reveal what the man had actually confessed to him, and without remorse. Ultimately, the girl rescues the priest in a way he'd been unable to rescue her earlier, and I have to say I was so moved that I burst into loud sobs in the tiniest screening room at Angelica, and couldn't stop—not that anybody else was dry-eyed, Victor included. After that, we met Helen for dinner, where I insisted on wearing dark glasses because suddenly I'd developed a migraine. She was concerned, but not at all surprised, she said, at the power of art to sicken ... or, conversely, heal.

When Victor and I chose the next movie, in midsummer, I voted for a documentary, with hopes of it being less emotional. In part, this would prove to be true, because somehow made-up lives could be you in a way that actual lives are not—a paradox. On the other hand, in this era, the truth was hard to top: for example, the home-movie-style film we saw about some ballot measure out in Oregon, the year before, launched by fanatical Christians against lesbians and gay men. I couldn't tell if it was good news or bad, but I suspect bad, that the largest block of people voting against the discrimination were sixty-five years and older. Luckily, that age group has a longer life expectancy than they used to, though that's the kind of joke you can make, sitting among free-thinkers, munching popcorn in the heart of downtown Manhattan. The most horrible part was two people getting blown up by a Molotov cocktail—it went that far, but why wouldn't it?—and the fact that the statewide referendum almost passed. So much for escaping emotion.

Our choice for the current afternoon, when Victor and I narrowed it down, was between the movie made from a play about the gay man who won't have sex, and another about a rich-girl/poor-girl romance. Old plot with a new twist: gorgeous teenage lesbians. Notwithstanding Oregon, times had changed and would continue to. I told Victor to hang up so I could call both theaters and find out the show times. He did, and after listening to the recordings, I dialed him back.

"Actually, I'd rather see the one about the man who won't have sex," I told him, when immediately he picked up the phone.

"Don't you think it's time we saw something about women?" he asked. "Though the documentary was mixed, let's not forget about the priest in June." We were continuing the conversation as if there hadn't been a gap, as if we'd never hung up at all. This was the way Victor and I always spoke.

"Yes, but who loved the priest? Who got a migraine from the priest?" I reminded him.

"It's true," Victor agreed.

"Because that film was about a person's moral stance in life, being able to love others, the brutality against girls and women who nonetheless can regain their power, and also about being gay," I told him. "I hate those party-line films that paint things so simply, as if all people, gay or straight, weren't incredibly complicated."

"But you don't know what that movie about the girls is going to be like," Victor chastised me.

"Oh, I'm not talking about that film in particular," I said. "And in fact, I would like to see something about women. But I can't honestly say I'm up for a story about teenagers. Their romantic crises don't interest me at my age."

"They don't?" Victor asked. I could hear a silence on the other end of the line before he added, "Me either, actually." So we decided on the one about the celibate man, who, I secretly thought, didn't sound all that promising himself.

By the time I finished walking over to the Quad, I was a few minutes late. After one of the hottest Julys on record, August had cooled down some, and I'd lingered on the way, in spite of myself, taking in one of the most beautiful days of summer. Still, I hated to keep Victor waiting in places I wasn't sure he could sit. So I arrived a little out of breath. But, as usual, he'd taken charge of the situation, having bought a ticket and plunked himself down on that odd carpeted thing they have there ... not really a bench but something like a platform you'd build into a stage set. Practically no one was in the lobby, so after handing me his cane, then grabbing my arm to stand, Victor began to make his way up the aisle while I went back for my ticket.

Though they weren't seating people yet, the usher had let Victor in anyway, and then me, too, when he found out we were together. It was like having attained instant VIP status, but at a cost that's not worth paying. Victor's long legs were difficult to control now, particularly on stairs, which he was climbing at that moment in front of me. This time, he'd handed his cane to the usher. There was no embarrassment or apology on Victor's part, like those people you see in wheelchairs who are singularly unimpressed by the people on a bus who keep looking at their watches while the driver sets up the hydraulic lift. On the other hand, he seemed appreciative of the help. I thought how Victor's illness had brought him closer to people ... after a period when he'd hardly talked to even his friends, except to yell at them. He'd been furious, and who wouldn't be?

"So what's your psychic film-critic forecast?" I asked Victor, as we settled into a row midway down the rake. I let him have the aisle seat, as I always did when we went to the movies, so that he could stretch out his legs.

"Well, I assume it will have the usual problems of a play made into a movie," he answered. "But also, it had problems as a play."

"You might have told me ahead of time that you saw it on the stage," I said. But it was more an afterthought than an accusation. And there's something about sitting in a movie theater in the afternoon, when it's daylight outside, that's pleasurable all by itself, no matter what you're about to watch. I settled back against the headrest, happy to be with Victor in the artificially induced twilight.

The rest of the audience started entering the theater. There were few enough people, men for the most part, that they filled the seats sparsely, talking a little, squeaking the chair bottoms with their bags and bodies.

"How romantic," Victor commented, pointing to a pair of boyfriends, two seats in front of us. They were utterly ordinary, with beefy necks and button-down shirts, though it was the way one suddenly placed his arm along the curve of the other's shoulders that Victor had referred to. That's when the movie started, and I have to say that, after it was over, I'd seen no emotion equal to the intensity of what we'd witnessed, in passing, between the two men in the audience. Not that it had meant to me what it had to Victor. I had no visceral reactions to men's bodies in that way; women had lived in my fantasies, and in my bed, all my life. It's just that public gestures once associated, by necessity, with privacy had an important meaning for all of us now.

"Was that a good movie in any way?" Victor asked, as we waited for people to clear the theater. He often liked to discuss things in the form of questions, as if he were conducting a survey.

"No," I said, putting an end to any soul-searching, at least on my part.

"Other people seemed to like it," he mused, referring, I think, to all the laughter from the audience. "On the other hand, the premise is completely unbelievable … that a healthy gay man would stop having sex because of AIDS."

"Unless he had a specific psychology or even phobia, which is not how this character was portrayed," I added.

"So then, does a movie have to be psychologically credible to work?" Victor continued his game of Twenty Questions.

"Of course not," I answered again. "But it does have to be

dramatic. For instance, if you believed at any point he might actually give in and have sex, which you don't, until at the very end, of course, when you know he will. After that dead friend appears to tell him the message of the movie and all of life—like Ethel Merman in *Gypsy*—to believe in those roses, whether or not they'll ever really come up."

"But isn't that just why the audience loved it?" Victor asked.

"I suppose so," I said. "But it's a tired theme by this point, and God knows Merman did it better."

By this time, the usher was hovering over us with a broom and dustbin. The next show was about to be seated. After negotiating the stairs—going down was harder than going up—Victor took my arm and we excused our way through the 6:30 crowd, which was substantially larger than ours had been. Victor said he needed to go to the men's room. So I led him to the doorway.

"Do you want me to come in with you?" I asked. I was kidding, which took him about a second to register. Then he disappeared inside.

Victor emerged a few minutes later, smiling before taking my arm. "The things I used to do in toilets," he reminisced. This made me think about the other things gone by the wayside, too.

Once on the sidewalk, I looked at my watch. We were supposed to have met Helen nearly fifteen minutes before, at a restaurant whose name and location none of us knew, exactly. Though it was just a few blocks away on Sixth Avenue, we were sure, I asked Victor to stop, which he did, leaning on my shoulder, so I could turn on my cell phone. It rang immediately, startling both of us. The call turned out to be from Helen, on her cell phone.

"I'm here," she said. "But it can't be the right restaurant, because Victor would never go anyplace called Hawaii Joe's

Bistro. Not that we would, either."

"It's Helen"—I turned to Victor—"and she's at Hawaii Joe's Bistro. That's not it, is it?"

"I don't see how it could be," Victor said. The confusion was this: he and I had eaten there when it had been a different restaurant under a different name, and neither of us could remember the exact address.

"We'll find it, and I'll call you right back," I told Helen. "Stay put." But after I hung up I realized I had no idea where she was, either.

Ironically, Victor and I found the restaurant just around the corner, between 12th and 13th Streets. We squeezed past a very crowded bar of smokers, emerging to a dining area in the back, where, because it was still early, we had our choice of tables. But when I called Helen again, her cell phone rang and rang, without her picking up. My own was always losing its charge, or I would forget how to deprogram it for theft of services. But not Helen, whose job as a video editor centered around her relationship to a complicated digital computer. I wondered if she'd gone out of range, and, if so, where. You forget how hostile technology is to geography.

Now that Victor was seated on the banquet and relatively comfortable for someone with almost no remaining meat on his tailbone, or anywhere else for that matter, I went off to find her. I figured she had to be within a block or two, but in my mind this had become a much larger landscape, the way internal space will expand or contract at will. On the street, I began to run, feeling ridiculous but unable to slow down, like a woman who's afraid that if she doesn't get to the train on time, her lover will have boarded it and left for points unknown. Just why these feelings came over me at that moment, when I knew she was so nearby, was a mystery. But I felt as I had when we'd first met, and at many times since. This had always been my experience of sexual love, a search that was never satisfied.

Suddenly I saw Helen up ahead—her firmly planted body, her dark curly hair, that remarkable concentration on her face as she stood looking through the door of the magazine store on 10th Street. I kept running and, when I reached her, didn't stop. She smiled, enjoying but not quite understanding the intense physicality of my arrival.

"Your telephone didn't ring," I said, as if this explained it.

"Damn," Helen answered, "I'll have to read that pamphlet again." But she didn't seem the slightest bit perturbed, as if she knew I could be counted on to find her, with or without any phone. Obviously, this was true, at least within a two-block radius.

Once all together at the restaurant, which turned out to be Moroccan, the three of us relaxed. The summer was nearly over, I reflected, and after Labor Day, school would start again. The romantic problems of teenagers, which I had avoided that afternoon, would then become my daily fare. Not that I minded in this context. College students were the most and least romantic of beings, part of the reason I loved teaching them. They were both bitter and hopeful … like the rest of us, I suppose.

"I wonder if *I'll* ever have sex again," Victor posed one of his usual questions after our appetizers had arrived. He was referring to the movie we'd just seen but also to his own physical condition.

"Don't count anything out," Helen said. I thought this was good advice, in general, though in my heart I didn't think he would have a lover after Ed, or even a pick-up, what with IVs in the morning, his gaunt physical appearance accentuated by a 6'3" height, the shirts he had once had pressed so meticulously now worn unstarched and untucked. On the other hand, his hair, shaved during the chemotherapy, had grown in nicely, and some gel gave it height and body. In fact, he had come back, nearly miraculously, from the winter before, his trademark leather jacket suspended then from his shoulders like some carapace a beetle might soon shed. But, aesthetic considerations aside—or maybe they weren't, maybe they were just practical, the way people's bodies are simply the mass through which we exist in time—he had accepted the love of his friends once more. And a transformation had taken place, however the rest of his life might unfold.

"This really is a handicapped-friendly city," Victor said, after a quickish trip to the bathroom, right after that. Luckily it was near our table, and the waitress had acted as tour guide. "That's one thing I notice now," he stayed with his thought. That night was the first time I'd heard Victor use the word handicapped in regard to himself or anyone. "For instance, when I had to meet Chloe at the movie this afternoon, it was at that strange hour, around 4:30 or 5:00, when suddenly there aren't any cabs. But an off-duty one stopped for me."

"The shifts change then," Helen said. "The daytime drivers are going off duty, but their replacements haven't taken over yet." It was the kind of information that, smart as he was, Victor never would have figured out, but Helen, as a union member, would know.

"Plus, I think Moslems pray around that hour, and most of the recent taxi drivers are from the Middle East," I added. Helen looked at me, as if to imply I was hardly an expert on Islamic religious practices, which was true. Still, I thought I was right and intended to look it up in my encyclopedia when we got home.

"At any rate," Victor went on, "I told the driver his off-duty light was on, figuring it was broken and he didn't know. But he said that, yes, he had been off duty and on his way to the garage, only I didn't look exactly mobile, so he'd decided to take me for his last fare. It turned out his daughter had some problem with her own legs."

LINSEY ABRAMS

Helen, as a native New Yorker, was not the slightest bit surprised by this act of good samaritanism. She nodded vigorously, as if everyone in the city could be counted upon to act this way, which, of course, wasn't true. Victor, for his part, kept shaking his head, as if it were closer to an act of God than a detour by a driver on his way home. And this wasn't quite true either. On the other hand, I thought each of them had a point.

Soon after that, we did the things you usually do in leaving a restaurant, only it took us longer—we paid the check, passing through the dining room, which was crowded now, then along the smoky corridor-like bar to the front door. Outside, we walked downtown a ways, to exercise Victor's legs, though it was painful for him. He even let out a little yelp once, like a puppy. Still, the evening was clear and cool, and a lot of people had left for their end-of-August vacations, so that the sidewalks were unusually open for the Village. It was pleasant to be out in the air.

Not long after that, Helen and I put Victor in a taxi. Then we hailed one for ourselves. After our friend's treatment that afternoon, I felt particularly fond of cab drivers and greeted ours like some long-lost friend. A diminutive man, he was responsive, periodically smiling into the rearview mirror. As we'd gotten in, I'd seen a bumper sticker on his fender that said *Read the Koran*, and I resolved to ask him, if it seemed appropriate later, just when Moslems did pray.

Helen gave him our address and asked him to take 8th Street across, before immediately pulling out her cell phone.

"Call me up," she said, "and I'm going to see if it rings now." She lifted the phone to her ear, waiting.

I thought this was ridiculous, both of us sitting cramped in a cab like that, but I didn't say so, because you learn to keep quiet sometimes after you've been with someone that long. I leaned as far as I could toward my side of the seat, even sticking my head out the window, while Helen pressed herself against the opposite door. With some difficulty, I dialed her number. But it still didn't ring.

"Could you turn on the light back here?" Helen asked the driver, reaching into her bag then slipping the directions from a Filofax overstuffed with pages.

"Certainly, madam," he replied, sounding like a servant from one of those really racist old movies, though they did have great atmosphere. It was his diction, along with the accent.

"Okay, try it again, Chloe," Helen told me, after having punched a series of keys on her phone. And this time it rang loud and clear. For some reason, she decided to answer it.

"Watson, come here ... I want you," I responded to Helen's hello. "Those were the first words that Alexander Graham Bell, who invented the telephone, spoke to his assistant," I told the driver, who I thought might not know.

"Yes, but a lot of people say that Bell stole someone else's research," Helen added, still talking into her phone, "and that he wasn't the inventor at all."

"Imagine such a thing," said the cab driver, lifting his eyebrows in the mirror. From his expression, I had the sense that he was doing just that, perhaps paying this fantasy more attention than the street in front of us.

"Let's hang up now," I suggested to Helen. But she wanted to talk longer on the phone, simply, I think, because it was possible. In that sense, she was a woman fully of the electronic age, in a way that I myself was not. In what I took to be an ironic gesture, though it may not have been, she started telling me about a man she knew who couldn't get anybody to listen to his poetry until he had the brainstorm of looping it on a synthesizer. Afterwards, he attracted huge audiences wherever he went and later made several CDs, becoming famous. While we talked, the driver kept looking over his shoulder, eyes narrowing. When the anecdote was finished, I finally persuaded Helen to hang up.

"Well, tonight has been a first, even for New York City," the driver suddenly announced to us. "You are, without a doubt, the most interesting passengers I have ever had in my cab." There was a rather dramatic pause.

"Really? What a nice thing to say," I told him, flattered in spite of myself. But Helen was taking the whole thing with a grain of salt, and had just finished putting her Filofax and phone back into her tote bag. "Though I doubt that could be true," I added, more modestly. "I mean, haven't you ever picked up any ... say ... celebrities?" I was thinking about Sydney and Donna Karan on page eighty-eight of *New York* magazine.

"Indeed, maybe I have," the driver answered. "But I'm isolated from the ways of this country, and I wouldn't know who any of them might be, even if he had sat in that very seat." He turned to peruse the back, once more taking his eyes from the street for just a little too long.

"You should get a television," Helen advised. She was starting to get involved, now, herself.

"Who has the time to watch TV? Who has the money for a set?" The driver posed his rhetorical questions in a way I thought reflected a greater knowledge of our culture than he'd let on. "You see, my life is in many ways a sad story," he continued, "because my father died when I was twenty and, as the eldest, all responsibilities fell on me. I had dreams of becoming something and someone else." The driver didn't say exactly what these dreams had been. But he didn't have to, because we've all had them, whatever they were.

"So suddenly I had my family to support. And I came to the U.S., where you find me here today."

He tossed his hands into the air, then gripped the wheel.

"Where are you from?" Helen asked the driver.

"Bangladesh," he replied. "I see my family once every year or two. But the worst part is this: I still miss my father dreadfully, and it's been almost eight years." Helen had lost her own mother at about the same age as the driver had lost his father, and I could see in her face that this endeared him to her—notwithstanding her feelings about Islam and its criminal treatment of women.

After that we turned onto Avenue A, home territory. When Helen and I remarked to each other about a new restaurant on the corner of 8th Street, the driver assured us he'd dropped off many people there and that they'd loved it. Just how he knew about their opinions coming out, as well as their expectations going in, was unclear. In fact, for someone so isolated, he seemed to have an enormous amount of knowledge about New York, and the East Village in particular—which clubs the "youth culture," as he called it, liked best, and which catered to which philosophical subgenres: skinheads, anarchists, college students. He pointed out a laundromat that the DEA had raided because of the heroin packets enclosed in the little boxes of free soap that came with every wash.

"No doubt, the cleanest junkies in America," the driver started chuckling, as if at a private joke. Helen looked at me, and it was true that his mood had grown increasingly odd.

As we approached the block where the squatters had been evicted, the light turned red and we stopped. There were plenty of people out, because in this neighborhood, as opposed to across town, vacations were taken not in Vermont or Italy but on the sidewalk. Weaving a little, a drunken and probably homeless man approached the taxi. The Bangladeshi seemed relaxed though vigilant, unlike many new immigrants who are particularly bigoted against African-Americans, which this man happened to be. We all watched him circle the car twice, picking up a more ebullient stride before returning to the driver's rolled-down window.

"You read the Koran?" the homeless man asked. He'd obviously seen the bumper sticker, too.

"Yes," said the driver.

"How's the plot?"

"The plot is good," the driver replied, sounding as polite and calm now as when we'd first entered the cab. By this time the light had changed, but we appeared to be going nowhere. There weren't any cars behind us, just a couple accelerating in the opposite direction.

"I mean, say, compared to the Bible," the homeless man said.

"I've never read the Bible," the Bangladeshi confessed. That's when Helen looked over at me again, her eyebrows raised. But as far as I was concerned, this conversation was in keeping with the whole odd-ball ride, her phone call included. So I joined in myself.

"I've read the Bible," I spoke up from the back. "Parts of it, anyway, because it seemed too long to finish."

"That's what people say," the homeless man reflected.

"Well, I'm Jewish," Helen finally told them. I knew she wouldn't be able to stay out of it. "And we just read the Old Testament, which *isn't* so long ... compared to the whole thing, I mean."

"I guess that's why they say the Jews are so smart," the homeless man commented. This was somewhat of a non sequitur, but you knew what he meant. "I'm a Baptist," he declared himself, so I said I was Episcopalian. Now each of us was accounted for.

By this time, we'd sat through two lights, and the cab driver shifted into gear. We all said good-bye to the homeless man, who, letting go of the side mirror, had clearly exhausted himself. With the next green, the taxi began slowly to pick up speed.

Suddenly, the homeless man began cursing and waving his arms. "Allah's going to send you straight to hell," he yelled after us.

With a squeal of tires, the Bangladeshi braked, then stuck his head out the window.

"He already has," he called back into the night. "I'm a cab driver."

As we were paying for the ride, two blocks later, I leaned inside the plastic partition to the front seat. "Would you mind if I asked you a question about your religion?" I asked the driver. He replied that he wouldn't. "When do you pray?"

The Bangladeshi looked amused. "At dawn, noon, mid-afternoon, dusk, and after dark, too. That's five times a day."

"Nevermind Victor, I'm surprised anybody can get a cab in this city," Helen muttered in my direction. She was against all religions on feminist grounds, but this would add fuel to the fire.

"Madam?" the driver said. He assumed she'd been speaking to him, which under the circumstances seemed reasonable.

"Well, I was wondering if that didn't cut into your other activities," Helen slightly rephrased her remark.

"Oh yes, certainly," he answered. "But like my father's early death, this tin can of a cab, that poor man on the street … it's a fact of life, now isn't it?"

Both Helen and I nodded, and of course the driver could see us in the mirror, because, though we were stopped, it was clear by now that he hardly ever kept his eyes on the road. The truth was, he was entirely uncommitted to driving that cab, except in some metaphorical sense, like those car rides you have in dreams, where you end up places you could not have reached, logically, either in time or space, like one of Einstein's theoretical solutions, perhaps.

Soon, Helen and I were inside, putting down our bags, tossing sweaters aside, locking the door. With a handy remote, she activated the living-room TV into sound and color.

"That driver was stark-raving mad," she said, flipping to the news.

"Possibly," I answered.

"I'm surprised he didn't run us into a streetlamp," she continued.

"I know," I said. "He wasn't a very good driver ... though, luckily, he never went very fast."

"Plus half the things he told us weren't even true," Helen said, dropping herself onto the couch. "I mean, about the neighborhood." As a twenty-five-year resident of the East Village, I think this was what had offended her most, nevermind the driving.

"But that's poetic license," I spoke up for the right to make life over. "Who says everybody has to be so wedded to the truth?" I pointed to the television, where real-life stories were being meted out in one-minute sound bites. This was Helen's province, in temperament as well as fact, whereas mine was the make-believe of art.

I suppose that's when I realized I'd underestimated that movie Victor and I had seen. I starting thinking about Ethel Merman, actually—and that way she had in *Gypsy*, and with all of the songs she sang before and after, of making everyone think that they, too, could hit the high notes. It was like the driver making me believe, for a moment at least, that Helen and I were the most interesting people he'd ever had in his cab, and how he'd stopped and remembered, you might say, who the homeless man must have been. It was also like Victor envisioning the future any old way he might want to. Or Helen, on that ride, insisting on talking into her cell phone ... to me, right next to her, on mine. And me getting a migraine from a priest. Who knows what makes a person tick?

People say that theoretical physics is more like poetry than anything else, though I wouldn't know. Beautiful is how I've heard it described. So thinking about the day just passed, I decided that if those hours had needed a kind of solution, too, and they had, I would have entirely reimagined the results: uncompromising Victor's immune system, reversing the

Bangladeshi father's early death thus liberating his son, not to mention a stupendous upgrade for the homeless man. In a way, that was what the cab driver had been doing, on a small scale, on our eccentric tour up the Avenue toward home. I'll say this: I'd had a good time in his company, and I thought he'd had a good time in ours.

Wendy Counsil

Here I am at nine months, wearing a dazed expression
I still occasionally see in the mirror.

Wendy Counsil's stories have been published in *Ploughshares*, *San Jose Studies*, and elsewhere. Her poetry has been in issues of *The Cream City Review*, *Western Humanities Review*, *Free Lunch*, and others.

Counsil currently lives in California's central coast region, where she writes and hikes among the redwoods.

WENDY COUNSIL
Cider Mill

utumn was never a good time for us. Jay and I have suffered our worst moments in these months when the trees are flamed with color. In 1978, we had that terrible Sunday afternoon smoking hash with a friend at the Arboretum. I had gotten lost going to the restroom and hadn't been able to find my way back to The Hole for nearly an hour; the guys had forgotten about me and had gone home alone, only to get arrested when they ran a red light on Washtenaw. In October and November of 1981, when I was pregnant with Amy, Jay was sleeping with his new graduate assistant. In 1986, we separated for the whole season and reconciled, I think, more in a spirit of surrender to the pattern of our lives than from any feelings of forgiveness or love. Since then, there haven't been many good times, though the terrible times seem to have eased somewhat, too.

This autumn we are making an attempt to reconstruct a marriage of sorts. The first ten years, it was me who dragged Jay to marriage counselors; this time, it is Jay who has had to persuade me to apply myself to the task. I am weary, perhaps, from the years of failure, settled in the comfort of my mild misery, less fearful now of this twin loneliness than he. He says it was his fortieth birthday that startled him into caring; I suspect it was another failed affair with one of his young women at the U.

Today's outing is part of Jay's strategy of planned family recreations. Amy is an unwilling passenger in the back of the Honda. She lies sprawled over the gray upholstery, chewing her cuticles and reading a complimentary copy of a singles want-ad pamphlet.

"Here's one," she says. "'Single white female, twenty-six, Julia Roberts look-alike, great figure, wants a financially secure professional with a sense of style. Um, blah, blah, theater, dancing, dining out, weekends away.' Sounds perfect for you, Dad."

The muscles in Jay's jaw tighten, but he says nothing. Perhaps I am supposed to say something wise to my daughter now, but all I can think of to say is that I feel sorry for the woman writing the ad, who anticipates that her home life with her dream man will be so dreary that she already longs for weekends away from it. Such cynicism is a horrible thing for a young woman to suffer. It makes me wonder what my daughter, already far beyond cynical, will expect in ten years from the men in her life. If this marriage has aged me, it has aged Amy more quickly.

Jay steers the car around an older man who rides a bike down the rutted road. This road, like most of southeast Michigan, is perfectly flat; the man, dressed in jeans and worn flannel shirt, pedals slowly, though he still puffs with exertion as we pass by.

"When are we going to get there?" asks Amy, but not as if she cares.

"Soon," says Jay, with false heartiness.

That falseness once drove me to anger, to worse anger than I felt at the lies it masked. Nothing these days seems to make me angry, nor joyous, nor passionate in any way. Certain days I imagine I am no longer alive, but am in some colorless purgatory designed by a sardonic God.

Still, the trees outside the windows grow naked every winter; each spring they bud; in summer they cast their heavy shadows. Because the seasons change around me, I think I must still be alive. The trees are on their way towards death once again, their leaves the colors of blood and bile and old bruises.

"Where is it?" asks Amy. "Haven't we gone too far?"

As I turn my head to look at her, Jay says, "No, I think it's just ahead." Amy rolls her eyes at me.

I force myself to speak. "I think we've passed it, too."

"Turn around and ask that guy on the bicycle, Dad."

Jay hesitates before answering. Like so many men, he hates asking directions, hates admitting he may be lost. This is one of those things we fought about during the good times. Over the years, my arguments turned to loud sighs, then to quiet ones. Today I don't make a sound. "Good idea," he finally says, and turns around in the next driveway.

I look over at him as the dappled light skims across his face. He is getting wrinkled, but only at the corners of his eyes and mouth. I have deep vertical creases between my eyebrows, and I reach up to touch them, then check myself as Jay glances over. Our gazes lock for a second, slide away.

As we near the bicyclist, I wonder what may have led the old man to be out here on this painfully sunny October day, so slowly and awkwardly pedaling down the back road. The man is somewhat beefy, and on the basis of that, I imagine a life for him, one in which he has had a heart attack and is forcing himself to follow the cardiologist's instructions about exercise. His plaid flannel shirt seems too heavy for the warm day. The shirt was once yellow, but it has faded now. I imagine that his wife keeps trying to throw out the shirt or donate it to the church rummage sale every autumn when she unpacks the winter clothes, but that the man loves the shirt, refuses to give it up despite its having worn out its usefulness. So when he goes on his daily bike ride, he puts on the shirt to save it from his wife's efficiency.

"Wave your hand out the window or something so he knows to stop," Amy says, and Jay does.

When Jay pulls up beside the man, the bicyclist looks grateful for the rest. I wait for Jay to speak, but he only rolls down his window and glances to me. I lean over Jay and smile through the car window, smelling warm asphalt. "Could you tell us where the cider mill is?"

The bicyclist ducks his head to look at me. "Up the road, past the blacktop, and the next road is it. Warren Road. Turn right."

"Thanks," I tell him. "I must have missed the turn."

The man says, "My wife's not a very good—what do you call it?—navigator, either."

I smile. "I'm not his wife. I'm his girlfriend."

Amy calls, "And I'm her sister."

"Oh," says the man, mildly confused.

Jay rolls up the window and looks at me with an awkward smile. Haltingly, he pats my knee, leaving a damp warmth. It's the sort of touch he hasn't practiced in such a long time that I suppose he's forgotten how. It's odd that it makes me smile now—not the pat so much as his clumsiness.

"I might like being your sister," says Amy.

"Okay. We can be sisters the rest of the day," I tell her.

When we get to the cider mill, there are hundreds of people in line. There's a line to watch the apple presses in action, a line to get on the pick-your-own-pumpkin hayride, a line for the retail sale of caramel apples and cinnamon doughnuts and plastic jugs of cider. We decide on that line; it's the shortest. We stand amid the cloying smells of fresh cider and frying doughnuts.

I watch the crowd as Amy picks out people to poke fun at. Around us are mostly young couples with small children, many fussing. There is no one here Amy's age, and that seems to help make her more comfortable. There's none of the slinking posture that means she's trying to hide the fact of her parents. "Look how pregnant that lady is," she says, pointing.

I look. There's a small-framed woman near a barn who is surely within days of delivery. A pink maternity top is tented over the baby, still riding high under her breasts.

Suddenly I remember the day fifteen years ago that I woke up to find Amy had dropped. It took all day to learn to walk again, readjusting to the shifted balance of the load I was carrying. Jay had broken off his affair by then, and I had let him get close to me again because I was so afraid. I knew that I couldn't afford to be a mother alone. That morning, I had stood up and he had stared at the change in my belly with child-wide eyes, the same pure green that Amy's eyes are. He had pointed and said, "Good God!"

"Yeah. It moved."

"There's a baby in there," he said in awe, as if he were just figuring it out.

Hope had risen in me then. I hoped that maybe the baby would change things, make us a family in a way we hadn't been before. Maybe with a baby, a child, a young person in the house, Jay wouldn't want to go away anymore.

It hadn't happened that way. And most days, I think I wasn't a very good mother to Amy, either, but that thought no longer frightens me as it once did. This surly, smart-mouthed young woman with the six piercings per ear and the dyed-black hair is not the child I had envisioned for myself—is not, in fact, any child I had envisioned, ever.

But this child is standing in the cider line next to me now, watching the pink-shirted pregnant woman lean against the barn wall to catch her breath.

"Nah, that's not a baby," says Jay. "That woman is smuggling a pumpkin out of here."

Amy laughs, and I realize that it's the first real laugh I've heard out of her in weeks, maybe months. Her father is grinning at her, and she's grinning back. Their mirrored green eyes are, for this moment, connected.

I step back from them, from their moment. An eddy of wind swirls leaves around my feet, leaves the color of the fluid that was smeared over Amy when she was born, leaves the color of pumpkins and the bicyclist's worn shirt. As the leaves crackle, they release the scent of decay. The pregnant woman moves away from the barn into the arms of a handsome young man, who takes great care that she doesn't stumble. Above us all, a barren blue sky goes on and on and on.

*Siobhan Dowd and Jake Kreilkamp—program director and coordinator,
respectively, of PEN American Center's Freedom-to-Write Committee—write
this column regularly, alerting readers to the plight of writers around the
world who deserve our awareness and our writing action.*

One Hundred Thirty-Four Iranian Writers
by Siobhan Dowd

For those of us in societies where picking up a pen can
have no consequences worse than a bad review, it can be hard
to envisage what those who are the subject of this column have
had to endure. If some writers are under the impression that a bad
review *is* a form a censorship, my advice is that they dwell upon
the following case of 134 writers in Iran, all of whom signed a
declaration calling for an end to censorship and who are now in
perpetual fear for their lives, since three have died, others have
been detained, interrogated, and threatened, and still others
forced into hiding or exile.

The current atmosphere has its origins in the 1994 death of Ali
Akbar Saidi Sirjani, a writer once featured in this column. Sirjani
had roundly denounced Iran's labyrinthine system of censorship
and the government responded by having him branded as an
"anti-Islamic" element in an official newspaper. He was then

arrested and accused of espionage, homosexuality, and drug usage (three stock charges for dissidents in Iran). Six months after his arrest, he mysteriously died in prison.

Horrified, a group of 134 writers issued an open letter to Iran's state-run press and to foreign news organizations, in which they stated the claims of literature as art, asking that their work be published and criticized on the basis of its own literary aims and merits, not prejudged by an ideological yardstick. "Writers must be free to create their work and express themselves," the letter said. "We are writers. That means we write and publish our sentiments, imagination, and thought. It is our natural, social, and civil right that our books reach readers freely and without any impediment." The state-run *Tehran Times* denounced the letter's writers as communists and demanded legal action against them, and the country's ayatollahs reportedly responded to the letter by accusing the signers of wishing to distribute pornography to children.

In October 1995, one of the 134, a highly regarded translator of Octavio Paz and Jorge Luis Borges named Ahmad Miralai, was found dead in an alley. The cause of death was reported as a stroke, and later as a heart attack, but the results of the autopsy were never made public. Recent reports from sources in Iran that must remain anonymous suggest that Miralai had a heart attack while being interrogated by the Information Office of the Revolutionary Forces. His interrogators apparently panicked when he had his seizure, injected him with a substance that caused him to have a stroke, planted a bottle of alcohol on him, and left his body in an alley.

Despite this incident, the writers continued to meet. Many of them received threats and warnings not to persist in their endeavor, but the wretchedness of not being able to write freely had convinced them to continue regardless. A new literary organization was planned, which would have had as the central plank of its platform a call for free expression. Their deliberations did not go uninterrupted. Some writers, meeting for dinner at the house of the German ambassador in Tehran, were taken away and accused of drinking alcohol. Others claimed to have been the victims of attempted murder while on a bus trip to Armenia. They reported that, while the passengers were sleeping, the driver leapt from the bus after putting it in neutral on a downward slope leading to a cliff. A catastrophe is said to have been avoided only because one of the writers was awake and able to slam on the brakes just in time. On September 12, another meeting was broken up by intelligence agents. All the group's materials were confiscated and twelve authors present were detained for questioning.

On November 3, Farraj Sarkoohi, a writer and editor of *Adineh (Enough)*, a prominent independent journal, disappeared while trying to leave Iran to visit relatives in Germany. He was last seen at Tehran airport, where he had reportedly met a member of the security services who had promised to help him with his visa requirements. For six weeks nothing more was heard of him, although there were rumors that he was sighted in the quarters of the Iranian intelligence agency, Vevak.

Eight days later, the body of another one of the original 134, Ghaffar Hosseini—a poet who divided his time between Paris and Tehran—was found in his apartment. Again, official reports claimed he had suffered a heart attack. However, this is belied by witnesses who saw the body, and said it bore signs of beatings. His apartment was subsequently sealed and none of his friends have been able to enter it to retrieve his writings. Both Sarkoohi and Hosseini were active organizers of the 134 and had been instrumental in delivering news of what is happening in Iran to dissident circles abroad. Both were also among the twelve arrested on September 12. The fate of Hosseini made Sarkoohi's friends, including his wife in Germany, all the more anxious for his safety.

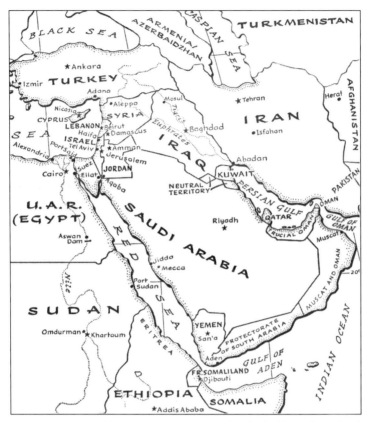

An international campaign on Sarkoohi's behalf was launched by the writers' association PEN. Radio interviews were broadcast into Iran, articles appeared in such newspapers as *Le Monde* and *The Washington Post*, and an open letter was signed by Edward Albee, Gunter Grass, Milan Kundera, Edward Said, and Susan Sontag. These efforts apparently bore fruit: On December 20, Sarkoohi reappeared at the Tehran airport, almost as mysteriously as he had disappeared. He told the press that he had been "traveling" to such countries as Germany (although the German authorities claim to have no record that he ever entered the country). When asked to produce his passport by way of proof, he said he had given it to someone else. He is now at his mother's home but is not allowed to leave Tehran. PEN continues to call on Iranian authorities to give him permission to leave the country.

The deaths of Sirjani, Miralai, and Hosseini, and the sinister disappearance of Sarkoohi has understandably chilled other members of the group of 134. Some of its most prominent members, including two of the country's most important poets, have left Iran, perhaps for good. Others are reported to be hiding. Letters requesting that the deaths of Miralai, Sirjani, and Hosseini be independently investigated, that those writers wishing to leave Iran be allowed to do so, and that all further supression of free expression be discontinued, can be sent to:

> His Excellency
> Hujjatol Islam Ali Akbar Hashemi Rafsanjani
> The Presidency
> Palestine Avenue
> Azerbaidjan Intersection
> Tehran, Iran

Brennen Wysong

Me and Snibby (my grandfather)—circa
March 1970—built for comfort.

Brennen Wysong is a native of West Virginia. He is currently working on his
MFA at Cornell University, and will be teaching there this fall. He is an
associate editor at *Epoch* magazine, and his stories have appeared in *High Plains
Literary Review*, *Story*, and *Alaska Quarterly Review*.

BRENNEN WYSONG
True North

*J*take my little girl to see the geese. There are two of
them, bedded deep in the wintering bitterweed edged along
Kitchen's Creek, their webbed feet drawn under their breasts,
unfolding themselves like a gift when Molly slams shut the
pickup-truck door. Their wings rise in Vs against the dusk.
Poised for flight, the birds slap their sides and send their drowsed
blood thudding through hearts no larger than change purses.
But the geese stay grounded. They remain anchored among
the parking lot's plowed drifts, making me wonder why this
Canadian Clipper, this cold front dipping down from the north,
doesn't drive them further south. I've often tried to imagine the
hand that drew these once-wild things from their angle, tamed
them with stale crusts and bruised fruit below the tipple of
Flatrock Consolidated Coke & Coal.

The hardened slush crunches under Molly's boots and my
voice rises in smoky gusts. Shhh. Hush. Careful. Up toward the
ridge's lip, men emerge from the mine shaft, lunch buckets
clutched in their fists, their blackened faces set against the snow
outlining the ragged slope of oak and poplar. I look for Bobby.
I expect to see his broad teeth framed in a grin, the look of a man
long too confident in himself, but then know better than to
believe he'll be there among the other miners. I recall a time

when I cupped his face in my palms. His eyes seemed furious with life as the rest of his expression faded away under the coal dust. I want the truth, I said. When his pupils darted into the corners of his eyelids, I was left staring at the full-blooded whites rimming his irises. The geese freeze in the deep tracks they've broken through the snow. Molly glances back at me, runs her weepy nose along the already slick cuff of her coat, across the wrist of her knitted mitten. Sometimes I hear Bobby's answer in the look of the child he'll never set eyes on again. I'm good as gone, he said.

The gate of the pickup thumps open above the bumper. Grasping the stiff plastic sack from the corner, I drag it across the truckbed and listen to it whisper against the metal. I work the graveyard shift at the bakery and coffee shop off I-19 now. Unwanted ryes and wheats lie piled like paving stones in the bottom of the bag. When I bend next to Molly, break the bread between my cold thumbs, I think of how I've gotten used to the routine that's left so little time between us. I think of the lumps of raw dough rising through the night, my wedding ring clicking against tin as I slap loaves from their pans, Molly waking herself for pre-school in the dark before I even make it home. It's me, I have to remind myself, the one bright spot in a family gone bad. Mama used to tell me how it would take more than a niece or nephew to set my brothers straight. You, she said, keep that Bobby away from them. The way he's feeling, the last thing he needs is to be running with the likes of them. But now I'm the one who stands with dough up to my elbows, listening for the hiss of the big diesel rigs' pistons in the parking lot. From the row of license plates screwed below their grillework, I can recognize the shapes of a dozen states and the hope promised in their mottos. I've read the bright signs on the trucks' hitches that warn travelers of explosives or corrosive materials. Not a nice night for driving, I'll say to them, refilling their coffee cups. I've realized how easily a wedding ring slips from a finger powdered with flour.

Molly unclenches her fist against the cold and slides her mittens over her rigid knuckles. One of the geese reaches for the bread she offers, a polished bill pecking her palm clean. It tickles, she giggles. I look for the slightest hint of fear welled in the eyes of these large, landed birds. With their tracks forming a semi-circle around her boots, Molly tries to touch the warm down smoothed along their undersides. I recall how they once came for the geese. Men from the Department of Wildlife and Natural Resources unfolded a topographical map on the hood of their truck and folks gathered to watch them trace migratory patterns with their thumbs. After they had tangled the geese in nets, they tagged their legs with silver bands and drew blood from their breasts. The men drove the birds to a bald knob atop a high ridge. Waiting for a clattering angle to burst below the clouds, expecting their wings to open to the familiar calling, they finally abandoned the geese on the pine-studded mountain spine, only to find that the birds had beaten them back to Flatrock. Bobby once raved about catching them himself and driving a full thousand miles north. When I found him in the tool shed, rapidly coiling a rope over his elbow and shoulder, I struggled to lay him down on the ground and then held a compress to his fiery forehead. Dry grass spoke beneath his heels as he kicked up heat from the still-warm earth. Hold still, I said. Hold it down. Shhh. It'll make you better. The new medication had driven Bobby into a state of delirium. His vomit pooled in the scoop of my flowered skirt. Where an outline of Molly darkened the door's warped screen, a beetle thudded and clung to the wire weaving before slapping against the loosestrife curling against the night. We had fallen that quiet, the three of us, my steadied breath against the firmest fear I'd ever seen set into Bobby's eyes. I watch a few miners hunched by the bumpers of their trucks and know how they share a last cigarette before heading home to their wives. I wave their way. Another time, Bobby swore, he'd empty enough buckshot into them to sink their bodies into Kitchen's Creek.

Squatted in the tangle of bitterweed, Molly collects feathers preened from the wings of the geese. She fills her hair and hands with quills, holds her arms out as if she too may take to flight. I think of the months before she was born, how Bobby still ran strong with my brothers—hulky, thick-knuckled boys who had a passion for killing, who set my husband's heart yammering like the wild bloody lumps within their own chests. Flushing pheasant from the brush at dawn, they watched the clumsy birds storm like large stones thrown across the sun. Clutches of deer crushed pine cones under their hooves and honed their antlers against the roots protruding through the loam. When my husband and brothers wandered in, drunk and hungry, the smell of smoke and still-warm death on their camouflage, I would think maybe this is what Bobby needs for a while, this man's kind of courage, these hard-driving ways, if he's going to keep on simply living. He would bury himself to the wrist in viscera and stuff his own prizes. But the game he'd killed never came to look alive after he was finished with his taxidermy work. I pluck a feather from Molly's hair. Watch, I say, ruffling it against my palm. All the fire, the piss and vinegar that once boiled in Bobby, floods Molly's cheeks, making me wonder what of him continues to live on in her. Behind my spine, my fingertips zip the feather's filaments back into a clean gray blade. Magic, I say as I hold it before Molly, tempted to show her how I've performed my little trick. But I just gather up her hair, push the quill through a tight bun, locking the feather in place with a twist. I think Bobby finally came to believe that life requires more than just magic. He understood that it takes more than an endless series of tricks to fool the blood through our veins.

Golden eggs, Molly exclaims. She scrabbles up the snowy banks and scours them for proof that fairy tales are true. I think how Molly has gotten to the age where nothing can be taken for granted. How can God, she once asked me, hold up all the stars in the sky at once? Maybe when people die, he makes each one of them do a little of his work. There are times when I believe myself no less a dreamer than she, equally vulnerable to doubting what I've dreamed. Leaned over the coffee counter at night, I've raked my tips from the Formica, turned the silver over in my palm, and discovered the image of an elk or schooner or beaver etched into metal dulled by a thousand fingertips. I keep these Canadian coins in my locker, wondering what I'll end up doing with them, telling myself I may in fact one day go there. Truckers have sent me postcards from states known for little more than their cornfields and I fear what words Molly's tongue shapes from their pinched script. I remember a clump of Queen Anne's lace, the stems clipped ragged with a fingernail and tied with twine, the petals floating in a jelly jar after the crowns had shed their white pinpoints, and I fear I've forgotten the hand that once offered them to me. Maybe even Bobby clutched them in a snowy field before they wilted and closed up as tight as the fists of infants.

Like Molly, I too turn over stones at the edge of the creek, cracking the thin sheet crusted against the rapid babble. The water shows signs of run off from the coal humped at the base of the tipple. Swirling a length of staghorn sumac in the water, I dredge the red sediments up from the muck and watch it fleet downstream. A ten wheeler rumbles down the road toward the power plant. Every electric light in town, Bobby once said, is powered by the coal harvested from the mine. Under a night sky roiling with storm scud, Flatrock lay in the valley like a world upturned, a scattering of stars, constellations that only we could cluster, connect into the stories of heroes and beasts. The first drop of rain slapped against Bobby's polished skull. Lightning split the ridge. Come Hell or high water, Bobby said, I'll be damned if I don't beat this thing. We sealed tight the windows of the truck, listened to the rain tumbling down against the roof in muffled gusts. Bobby's body, hairless as a child's, bone white in the glow of the radio dial, moved above me as I arched my spine, the blades of my back slowly sucking away from the humid plastic seats. When a country song on the radio crackled with static, my eyes broke open and flushed tears from the corners of my lids. I caught the strike of lightning, its flash swirled in the rain washing down the windshield. In that quick brilliance, I noticed one of Bobby's last eyelashes pasted to his sweaty cheek. Make a wish, I said, touching my fingertip to it, blowing it away.

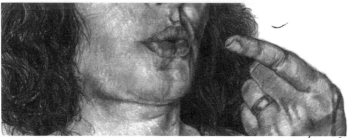

J. LEON 97-

Molly bends behind one of the geese. Do golden eggs hatch into golden goslings? she asks, following the bird as it spreads its wings and lets out a grinding honk against these hills. The goose releases its bowels and dumps its steaming feces in the snow. Seeing how the cold cusps Molly's ear, pinkening its curve, I wonder if the tips of her fingers and toes have turned numb. I worry about her more now than I ever have. I recall all of Bobby's recklessness, how Molly had to live through it those first few years of her life. Days before we had to rush off to the hospital, Bobby and my brothers emptied their rifles in the passive flanks of a milking cow pasturing in a field. The pickup bucked up the rutted front drive, the engine thundering under the truck's weight, the wheels spitting cinders against the house's aluminum siding. The Guernsey's fawn-colored coat appeared freshly painted red in the moonlight. It seemed slick, as if dipped in crude oil, the massive holes blown through its hide still leaking a deep crimson. With their drunken voices cursing and laughing, they dragged the cow up to the shed behind the house. I'll always remember believing how there would be no way to bring Bobby back after something as outlandish as this needless killing. Earlier in the week, the doctors had run more tests on him. His cancer, once the size of buckshot pellets, enlarging into a series of black constellations, had spread and begun to pump rapidly through his blood. In the rectangle of light, I watched Bobby split the cow's belly down to the udder. I winced as the still-warm milk struck his gory hands in a splash and instantly pinkened across his knuckles. Molly would be born within a few days of that evening. Lying back down to bed, I weaved my fingers below my rounded belly and imagined Bobby fully opening up the Guernsey. To make his next cut, he would need to crawl deep inside her rib cage, only to realize that his own rifle had taken any chance of finding the mystery hidden behind her heart.

Molly begins to tease the geese and I think how a child's play can eventually turn for the worse. Stop it, I say, harsher than I'd expect. She spins around, laughing, the feather shed from her bun, her hair showering over her shoulders, before she chases after them again. The geese slide on the ice as their wings rise against the darkening drifts. But I know no amount of cruelty could ever untame them. Daddy's little girl, I think, wondering what blood is not tainted by a disease that drives a once-strong man wild with pain. One afternoon while Molly played in the front yard, I broke the breach of Bobby's rifle with a creak from its gritted hinge, ran my fingers over the floral-like patches of rust blooming over the unoiled gunmetal. I tested the barrel against my mouth, the bitter bite of steel on my lips, my tongue, trying to understand what brings a man to such a moment, then realized my arms didn't stretch far enough to reach the trigger. C'mon, I say to Molly. Let's get going, I tell her as I open the pickup-truck door. The headlights flare across the geese like a misleading beacon, catching them in a bright arc as Molly runs through the snow toward me. 🪆

Pete Fromm

*This is the earliest photo I have. My mother made
the papers: "Little Woman Does Things in a Big Way."
My brother and I weighed in at just under nine pounds each.
A day later Paul had managed to get over the excitement,
but I'm still wide-eyed in amazement.*

"Six Inches of Water" will be included in Pete Fromm's newest collection, *Dry
Rain*, from Lyons & Burford. His other books include the story collections
The Tall Uncut and *King of the Mountain*, the novel *Monkey Tag*,
and the autobiographical *Indian Creek Chronicles*, winner of the Pacific
Northwest Booksellers 1994 Book Award. He lives in Great Falls, Montana.

PETE FROMM
Six Inches of Water

*L*eaning close, nearly touching Duncan's face, Mickey couldn't stop himself from looking for a glimpse of Carol. But the warmth of his son's breath touched Mickey's cheek, and, closing his eyes, Mickey released the seatbelt and eased Duncan from the truck without waking him.

Cradling Duncan's head against his shoulder, Mickey turned to the rented beach house, wondering if there were another child in America who would volunteer to skip the plane ride, who would say he'd rather drive even after Mickey sat him down with a map, showing the distance from Laramie, Wyoming to Ocean Beach, New Jersey.

"From our home to our vacation," Duncan had called it.

At the time Mickey worried that the distance and time were incomprehensible to a six year old, but through the four hard days on the road Duncan had sat for hours staring out the window at everything they passed, even when it seemed for hours they passed nothing. He slept sitting up, napping like he hadn't in years. It was Mickey who pestered Duncan about stopping to eat, about stopping to pee, not the other way around.

When Duncan talked it had been in long spurts: about his

friends, about seeing the ocean. Late the first day he asked, "Did Mom ever see a ocean?"

Mickey had stammered, "No," then, "She was from Wyoming." When his son kept looking at him, kept waiting, Mickey'd pointed at whatever they were passing, asking, "Have you ever seen anything like that, Dunc?" It was something ridiculous, a fence or something, and Duncan hadn't bothered answering. And he hadn't brought up Carol again for a long time.

But, at the end of every day, when they pulled into the night's motel, Duncan made Mickey promise that they weren't moving to New Jersey, even though it's where all his uncles and aunts lived, his grandparents and cousins. He made Mickey promise that as soon as the vacation was over they'd go back home to Wyoming, where they'd always lived. Mickey wondered if he'd listened in on his parents' calls after Carol's funeral: "There's no reason anymore, Mickey, for you to be so far away."

Now, in the predawn gloom, Mickey carried Duncan down the skinny walkway between the tightly packed vacation homes. When he'd called yesterday, his parents had told him how excited the whole family was to see the two of them; that they'd leave the door unlocked if he really thought they had to come in the middle of the night.

It was closer to dawn than the middle of the night, but they'd made the last haul through the night, Mickey wanting Duncan back on schedule for his family. He didn't want any scenes now, everyone else already together long enough to discuss his situation, ready to look for signs anywhere, even in Duncan, to betray the hardships.

The rust-hinged screen screeched, and Mickey stretched Duncan out on the narrow bed. Taking a step back, he sat on the made-up cot. He watched Duncan sleep, open mouthed the way Carol had. He lowered his face to his hands, rubbing his stubbled cheeks, exhausted beyond sleep.

But he tried, swinging his legs up on the cot, feeling in the first moment how the center bar would cut into his back. The cot, he knew, was meant for Duncan, and tonight Duncan would fight him for the novelty of it. Fight and win, Mickey thought. He lifted his arm over his eyes, glancing at his watch. Quarter to five in the morning.

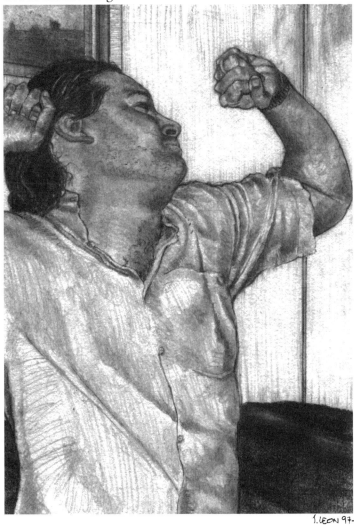

Within a minute the skin of Mickey's arm and forehead was slicked with sweat. The air was heavy and briny, something he'd almost forgotten in the high dry of Carol's Wyoming. Mickey sat up, blowing out a long, quiet breath.

Scattering T-shirts and underwear across the cot until he found his swim trunks, Mickey slipped out of his shoes and jeans. He stood to slip on the trunks, but caught his foot and crash-landed back on the cot. He sat there naked, his foot caught in the neon blue nylon, and saw Duncan watching him, three feet away.

"Go back to sleep," Mickey whispered, tugging at the trunks. "Excitement's over. Nothing to see here."

"Are you going swimming?"

"Just hot," Mickey lied, glancing at his watch again.

Duncan had been sleeping since Pittsburgh. Seven hours. Though Mickey'd thought of actually being alone, of walking into the water with no one to watch, even of the beautiful fuss his parents would make over finding their grandson when they woke, he couldn't help asking, "Want to?"

Duncan shot up, wriggling out of his jeans. He was already wearing his trunks, like underwear.

Mickey blinked. "When did you put those on?"

"At the motel. I never swam in a ocean before. I never even seen a ocean."

Pulling two towels from the folded stack, Mickey said, "We'll still be back before anybody gets up."

Duncan took hold of two of Mickey's fingers, a habit he'd revived in the year since the funeral, and they walked the twisting little streets together, Duncan dropping his hand often enough to pick up a stick or broken bits of sea shells. He threw the stick into a dead-end waterway identical to the one bordering their cabin, bristling with pleasure boats. "What's the ocean going to be like?" he asked.

"Big."

"How big?"

"Huge."

"How huge?"

Mickey blew out a breath, swinging through a circle, looking for landmarks in the flat crowd of mechanically quaint houses. Lost now without mountains.

"How huge?" Duncan asked again.

"You'll see it in a second," Mickey answered, bending down and waving him over. Duncan ran holding out his arms and Mickey swung him onto his shoulders.

With his boy's legs clamped around his ears, Mickey walked almost an entire block before the next question. "Dad?"

Mickey sighed. "What, Dunc?"

"What's the Topic of Cancer?"

Mickey glanced at his hands, tight around Duncan's ankles. "What?"

"The Topic of Cancer. What is it?"

"Tropic," Mickey whispered. "I think you mean Tropic. It's geography."

"But it's in the ocean, isn't it?"

"It's only a line somewhere," Mickey answered. "Like longitude. It's nothing real."

"Oh, I thought maybe Mom went there."

Mickey looked out at the ocean, visible now between the last row of houses, a fog hiding the flat line of the horizon. "No," Mickey said, the word sticking in his throat. "I told you about Mom. It's not that kind of cancer. It doesn't ..."

"Oh," Duncan said, stopping him.

He carried Duncan down the path between the last of the beach houses, wondering what else he could say. But as soon as he stepped onto the sand, Duncan kicked his heels against his chest, squirming until Mickey could put him down. He ran toward the water, shouting, "Think it'll be warm?"

"I don't know," Mickey answered, stepping more quickly, the sand clutching at his feet. "Slow up. Wait for me before you go in."

But the flat sand, hard and wet beyond the reach of waves, was something different, and suddenly Duncan stepped more slowly. Mickey fell in beside him. The water itself was still and slick, barely lapping the edge of the beach. The red ball of the sun burned and wavered through the mist.

"I thought there'd be waves," Duncan said.

"There'll be some before we leave. You'll get to surf."

"I don't know how."

Mickey looked down at him, his bare feet making little prints in the damp sand. "I'll teach you, Dunc," he said.

Duncan asked, "How did it get wet all the way up here if there's no waves?"

"The tide must be going out."

"What's the tide?"

Mickey rubbed his forehead. "Something the moon does. The ocean moves up and down. Every day."

The boy glanced over his shoulder. "The moon?" he said.

Mickey reached for him, but Duncan jumped away, ripping down the tidemark, the sand as hard as a street.

Mickey let him run, thinking of the hours and hours trapped in the car, but then gave chase, closing in tight. Duncan shivered and giggled as Mickey touched his naked back, so close to really catching him.

Then Mickey dashed to the side, careening into the ocean. The water was much warmer than he'd guessed, nearly bathtub warm, and the sand did not deepen its pitch, but stretched out endlessly, leaving Mickey running through ankle-deep water, then knee deep, when he'd thought he'd be able to splash in and dive under before Duncan could react.

He heard Duncan splashing in behind him and Mickey was so proud of his chasing him right into something so unknown he had to fight the tears he'd kept back ever since realizing how badly they frightened Duncan.

"You can't get me!" Mickey shouted, but he was slowing and slowing, waiting for the touch of his son.

And when he felt the small hands, the nails that needed trimming, Mickey turned, catching Duncan and falling. Duncan followed him under, grabbing at his neck, his head. Even underwater, Mickey thought he could hear him laughing.

Mickey kicked away from the bottom, the sand out there as hard as it was on shore, and threw himself into the air, still holding Duncan tight. But Duncan only shouted, "I got you!" pounding his fists against Mickey's shoulders.

Then, abruptly, he stopped. "Yuck," he said, licking his lips.

"Salt," Mickey explained. He flipped Duncan onto his back, letting him loose. "Float," he said, and Duncan did, his eyes going wide at the new cork-like properties of his body.

He struggled up, the water making a line beneath his narrow chest. He gave Mickey his can-you-believe-what-we've-discovered stare, and said, "Let's go deeper."

And though they played the whole way out, when Duncan's toes suddenly lost their hold on the bottom, the water floating him free, he asked about sharks, turning back for shore before Mickey could answer. Mickey had to follow him in, saying there weren't any sharks here, there wouldn't be a beach if there were, they wouldn't allow swimming, it was perfectly safe.

"Nothing's perfectly safe," Duncan answered, trudging toward the empty beach.

Mickey stopped, then started after him again. "Come on," he said. "We can play here. Even if there were sharks, they couldn't swim in this far. It's too shallow."

"Sharks can swim in six inches of water."

"How do you know?" Mickey asked. Then, "There's no sharks, Duncan."

Duncan wavered, but kept going. He put his arms around himself. "I'm cold then," he said.

So they walked the beach, Duncan finding shell after shell,

asking for identifications Mickey couldn't give. "How come the water's salty?" he asked.

"All oceans are salty."

"How come?"

"Because they're the oceans. They're saltwater."

"How come?"

Mickey looked back to where they'd entered the beach, making sure he could remember the house. "Evapomass transpiration," he mumbled.

"Oh," Duncan answered, picking up the husk of a horseshoe crab. He sat down with it, scraping at the sand with the shovel-like shell. Mickey sat beside him.

Duncan dug his shell deep into the beach, quietly heaping up sloppy stacks of wet sand. "Dad?" he asked.

Mickey couldn't help rolling his eyes. "What, Dunc?"

"Do you even miss Mom?"

Mickey's mouth worked a second without making a sound. "What? Of course I do."

"Oh." He waited before asking, "Then how come you don't talk about her?"

Mickey reached out to smooth his son's wild hair, but it was dry already, salt-hardened spikes added to the tangle. Searching for something to say, he glanced at the sun, still a red ball, still something possible to look at, and suddenly the word *ovary* sprang into his head, and Mickey wondered if that's what Carol's had looked like, that overwhelming. "Dunc?" he said, just to keep from gasping.

"Huh?"

"You mind if I take a swim?" He took a breath. "You could build a big, huge sand castle. When I get back we can bomb it."

Duncan kept working, digging the moat. "I don't want to bomb it," he said.

"Okay. We can just keep building it, bigger and bigger. The

biggest ever." Mickey looked away from the sun.

"Okay."

"You'll stay right here? Like we've talked about? You won't talk to anyone?"

The boy glanced one way down the deserted beach, then the other.

"People will start coming. It's getting late."

Mickey stood up, stepping toward the water, looking away from the ball of the sun. "Really. Stay right here."

Duncan nodded, still digging.

"Dunc?"

"Okay, Dad!" he said sharply, still not lifting his head.

Mickey watched him a moment more. "I'll be right back. You can watch me."

"Okay."

When Mickey stepped into the water, his son finally looked up. "Watch out for sharks," he said.

Mickey walked farther out. He turned, raising his voice. "I can swim faster than any old shark," he said, wishing it were true. Any old cancer. "You know that."

"Nobody can do that."

"I can," Mickey yelled, "I'm your dad."

Duncan still watched him, doubting, and Mickey dove.

He swam beneath the surface as long as he could, biting his lips shut, the word *ovary* blinding. For Christ's sake, the Topic of Cancer. He swam hard, kicking against the water, lungs straining.

Not even bending over the hugeness of Carol's belly, talking to their child before they'd known he'd be a Duncan, not a Laura, were ovaries something they'd thought about. Not until the checkup, put off so long for so many perfectly good reasons, not until the biopsy came back with its sentence, did *ovary* become this word that could turn even the sun against him.

Mickey broke the surface at last, sucking in a huge breath. He heard a trace of Duncan calling, "Dad!" and he spun around, trying to stand but finding he'd swum too far. He went under for a second, then kicked high, seeing Duncan standing by his castle, waving at him. The ocean had picked up; long, slow swells easing toward shore, and Duncan disappeared as Mickey sank into a hollow.

He'd stayed under too long, Mickey realized. He swam onto the next swell and kicked up, waving again, shouting, "I'm okay. No sharks."

Duncan waved back and then disappeared behind the swell running out from under Mickey.

Mickey turned, swimming out again. He stroked carefully, remembering how Carol had moved in the water, like something born there, an otter or something. But she'd never seen an ocean herself, and now he was swimming in one alone, her boy making sand castles behind him.

Though he'd meant to parallel the beach so Duncan could watch, Mickey kept swimming straight away from shore. Without Duncan back there on the beach, he thought, he might keep swimming. Clear to the Topic of Cancer.

But finally Mickey stopped, rolling onto his back, his eyes closed against the sun's red ball, bobbing in the salt the same way Duncan had earlier, with something of the same wonder. Sometimes he cried only because he was so glad there was still Duncan, that he could keep him so tethered to shore.

He bobbed there longer than he knew, wishing they could finish this visit and then drive somewhere else, the West Coast maybe, see another ocean. Then go on to the next, somewhere new, somewhere salty, the Gulf maybe, never slowing enough to let anything catch up.

With the sun red-black against his closed eyes, a rolling swell lifted Mickey's ears above the water and he heard his name again, shouted across the sea. "Mickey!" this time, not "Dad!"

He turned slowly, wondering if he'd really heard such a thing,

142

and when he kicked up to look, he saw a crowd on the beach where he'd left Duncan, and his stomach came into his mouth, and he started swimming faster than he ever had in his life. Faster even than with Carol.

Though he could hardly breathe, he turned his head anyway, exhaling by screaming his son's name into the salty water he flashed through. With every lifting swell he pitched his head back, still swimming, but searching the shore, the little group huddled at the water's edge waiting for him. The salt stung his eyes and the group remained nothing more than a horrifying blur, and he cast his head back into position, his arms and lungs burning. Swimming for Duncan. For Carol.

The group grew rapidly, Mickey wondering if he'd last long enough to reach them. But the next time he looked, a tiny person broke free and dashed into the ocean, splashing toward him.

Mickey kept swimming, his head up, the rescue stroke he'd learned half his life ago. "Duncan!" he screamed, using breath he couldn't spare. He kept his head up long enough to hear "Dad!" then Mickey dropped his face back into the water, driving for the finish, and when he looked again Duncan was only yards away, and Mickey scooped him up, throwing him clear of the ocean and catching him before he could touch down.

"What happened? What?" Mickey gasped, staggering in the last of the swells, the water streaming from his eyes until he could see that the group there, the people Duncan had broken away from, was his family, all of them, standing on the sand at the edge of the water, some only in robes, all staring at him.

Mickey pried Duncan a few inches from his chest, looked at his face, struggled for breath. "What?" he asked. "What?"

"The sharks!" Duncan answered, sobbing, pushing his face back into Mickey's chest.

Mickey hugged him there, tottering toward shore, toward his family, shaking his head, asking with his eyes.

His mother stepped forward, shaking her own head, saying, "Mickey?" and nothing else, not *What in the world?* not *How could you?* nothing but "Mickey?" Then, "He was scared half to death."

Mickey hugged Duncan tighter, thinking what a sweet thing that would be; being scared only half to death.

"What happened?" Mickey asked again, reaching the sand, holding Duncan across his chest as he had when he was a baby.

His family opened for them, a half-moon pinning Mickey to the ocean's edge.

"He came bolting in like there was a fire," Mickey's father answered. "Everybody still in bed, him screaming, 'Sharks! Sharks! Sharks got Dad!'"

Mickey opened his mouth, but no words came. He glanced at his son, saw his eyes clamped tight, his cheeks burning red. He pictured the maze of streets, the identically cute cottages or bungalows or cabins, whatever they were called. He lifted Duncan as close to his face as he could.

"How in the world did you find them?" he asked.

Duncan bit his lip, twisting his face even farther to hide against his chest. "I remembered," he said, his voice stuttering over a sob.

"It's okay," Mickey whispered. "It's okay, Dunc."

Mickey took a step forward, saying, "I'm sorry," then saying it again. "Everybody, I'm sorry. It's just …" He stopped, swinging Duncan up to his shoulder, the way he used to burp him after the bottle. *It's just what?* he wondered.

"Okay," Mickey's father said, herding his clan away from the swelling ocean. "Excitement's over. Nothing to see here."

Mickey tilted his head against Duncan's, murmuring to himself, "You are the best baby in the world. And you've got the best Mommy ever. You are going to be …," the old burping mantra.

Duncan clung to him, shaking his head against his shoulder. "I don't want to live here, Dad. I can't remember Mom here."

"I promised, Dunc. Remember?"

"There's sharks here, Dad."

Mickey took a breath. "Your mom always wanted to see a shark. Did you know that?"

Duncan shook his head, turning just enough to look at him.

Mickey walked across the sand with his family. "She did," he whispered to his son. "She used to say I swam like a shark. Back when we first met."

"On the swim team?"

Mickey nodded. "On the swim team," he repeated. "Before you were even a tadpole." That was Carol's line, but Duncan only leaned against him, waiting to hear more.

The
Last
Pages

*Our father's father's mother, Eliese Bumann Burmeister,
just prior to her death at age eighty-one in September 1935.*

*B*irds occur again and again in my work. I often seem to drive them in flocks across my pages. Red-tailed hawks. Fighting cocks. Geese. I plan a piece on John James Audubon, the fact that he sold every-thing—save his gun, dog, clothes, drawings—the summer of his young daughter's death. Herein lay what he could still trust. I have imagined Audubon watching passenger pigeons storm

across the sky, eclipsing the sun, their dung like a snow squall, the beat of their wings a lolling buzz. He sees sports-men taking aim at a murder of crows. Chimney swallows pour forth for minutes from a hollow sycamore. An exalta-tion of larks. Audubon's hands are giants. They sketch birds, fill diaries and logs, giving shape to songs in drawings and words, and I try to be there to witness their every movement.

MARY OVERTON

*A*fter Life" is dedicated to the memory of Cleo, the Flying Nun dog. My sister Kathi gave Cleo that title because her ears looked like Sally Field's wimple in the TV show by the same name. In this photo, the shadow of her ears looks like the angel wings I am sure she now wears. Cleo was a spiritual creature, although not terribly bright, and my companion for six years. We took many long walks through the woods described in this story.

*T*his is a photo of my living room after the 1989 Loma Prieta earthquake. Despite having to occasionally pick up such messes, I love California's quakes. They help remind me that if the earth itself is so elastic and mutable, then nothing in the realm of human affairs can be all that difficult to change. (Also, to be less cerebral, the adrenaline rush that comes with an earthquake is kinda fun.)

PETE FROMM

My father took this picture on the back porch of that rented beach house at Ocean Beach. It was a family reunion, but my wife, Rose, couldn't make the trip east, so I was there on my own. We had no children then, so the dawn swim I took was a solo. The oddness of being alone in such a cluster of family worked on me until, a few years later, Duncan and Mickey tried the same thing.

LINSEY ABRAMS

*H*ere I am, over ten years ago, in the fall of '86, at Edith Wharton's house in Lenox, Massachusetts, touring her stone garden on the last day of the season there. This picture was taken by my lover, a woman I've lived with for fifteen years now. I think life—and stories—are really about what you do know, and don't know, at a given time. For example, that afternoon, I did know I would live with my photographer for the foreseeable future, though I didn't know how shamelessly I would introduce her into my work, too, at a later date. (See "The Theory of General Relativity.") I also didn't know that the novel I was working on then would end up in a drawer, a fiasco and a bitter creative defeat. I didn't know, either, that so many of my friends would be dead from AIDS within a decade. And yet, something about the photograph seems to imply what's ahead. I guess that's why I see my writer's role as documentarian, with license to lie. From that day at Lenox, there were happy pictures, too.

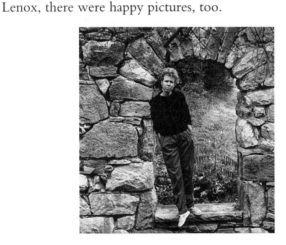

GREGORY SPATZ

I knew that I wanted Jeremy to emerge transformed at the end of "Stone Fish," and I knew that his transformation should reflect some of the ways he imagines himself on page one; but I didn't want the transformation to happen via conventional story action and narration. I wanted to use the more motionless connections the story kept giving me—water inside ice, sculpture inside stone, fossil inside stone, earth under snow, love inside silence, etc. I wanted to move things along narratively by making and breaking those sorts of connections, not by maintaining the usual circumstantial dramatic tensions. The language and surface of "Stone Fish" are all conventional enough because this is what I tend to like in stories—simplicity and clarity. It practically begins, "Once upon a time." But nothing really *happens* in the traditional sense of things happening in stories, and this is what made me crazy writing it, and what kept me wanting to continue.

*T*his is me with my nephew Derek. We're impersonating monsters in order to scare the real monsters away.

Derek and his sister Rachel, now four and five, are always making me go back to my own childhood and wonder, because they are such wonderers themselves. It's remarkable how vividly the two of them perceive. They're my teachers—and my pals.

KENT NELSON

The road smoothed out a mile or so past the Carrises', where new asphalt had been laid. I slowed to let the calm take hold, and the truck glided. The hills were shadows beyond the reach of the headlights, but I knew that road: I knew the bends and the swales and the hills. It was a country of my own making, and there were stories there, tales I had already dreamed, new worlds I intended to make of the passing of the seasons. In the far distance—miles away still—the solitary light of my own house appeared beyond the low hills, disappeared, reappeared again, trembling, it seemed, in the clean air, like a comet moving away from me even as I rushed toward it along the highway through the dark air.

—from "A Country of My Own Making"

*P*AST CONTRIBUTING AUTHORS AND ARTISTS
Issues 1 through 22 are available for eleven dollars each.

Robert H. Abel • Steve Adams • Susan Alenick • Rosemary Altea • A. Manette
Ansay • Margaret Atwood • Aida Baker • Brad Barkley • Kyle Ann Bates •
Richard Bausch • Robert Bausch • Charles Baxter • Ann Beattie • Barbara
Bechtold • Cathie Beck • Kristen Birchett • Melanie Bishop • Corinne Demas
Bliss • Valerie Block • Harold Brodkey • Danit Brown • Kurt McGinnis Brown
• Paul Brownfield • Judy Budnitz • Evan Burton • Gerard Byrne • Jack Cady
• Annie Callan • Kevin Canty • Peter Carey • Carolyn Chute • George Clark
• Dennis Clemmens • Evan S. Connell • Tiziana di Marina • Junot Díaz •
Stephen Dixon • Michael Dorris • Siobhan Dowd • Barbara Eiswerth • Mary
Ellis • James English • Tony Eprile • Louise Erdrich • Zoë Evamy • Nomi Eve
• Edward Falco • Michael Frank • Pete Fromm • Daniel Gabriel • Ernest Gaines
• Tess Gallagher • Louis Gallo • Kent Gardien • Ellen Gilchrist • Mary Gordon
• Peter Gordon • Elizabeth Graver • Paul Griner • Elizabeth Logan Harris •
Marina Harris • Erin Hart • Daniel Hayes • David Haynes • Ursula Hegi •
Andee Hochman • Alice Hoffman • Jack Holland • Noy Holland • Lucy Honig
• Linda Hornbuckle • David Huddle • Stewart David Ikeda • Lawson Fusao
Inada • Elizabeth Inness-Brown • Andrea Jeyaveeran • Charles Johnson •
Wayne Johnson • Thom Jones • Cyril Jones-Kellet • Elizabeth Judd • Jiri
Kajanë • Hester Kaplan • Wayne Karlin • Thomas E. Kennedy • Jamaica
Kincaid • Lily King • Maina wa Kinyatti • Jake Kreilkamp • Marilyn Krysl •
Frances Kuffel • Anatoly Kurchatkin • Victoria Lancelotta • Doug Lawson • Jon
Leon • Doris Lessing • Janice Levy • Christine Liotta • Rosina Lippi-Green
• David Long • Salvatore Diego Lopez • William Luvaas • Jeff MacNelly •
R. Kevin Maler • Lee Martin • Alice Mattison • Eileen McGuire • Gregory
McNamee • Frank Michel • Alyce Miller • Katherine Min • Mary McGarry
Morris • Bernard Mulligan • Abdelrahman Munif • Sigrid Nunez • Joyce Carol
Oates • Tim O'Brien • Vana O'Brien • Mary O'Dell • Elizabeth Oness • Mary
Overton • Peter Parsons • Annie Proulx • Jonathan Raban • George Rabasa
• Paul Rawlins • Nancy Reisman • Linda Reynolds • Anne Rice • Roxana
Robinson • Stan Rogal • Frank Ronan • Elizabeth Rosen • Janice Rosenberg
• Kiran Kaur Saini • Libby Schmais • Natalie Schoen • Jim Schumock • Barbara
Scot • Amy Selwyn • Bob Shacochis • Evelyn Sharenov • Ami Silber • Floyd
Skloot • Lara Stapleton • Barbara Stevens • William Styron • Liz Szabla • Paul
Theroux • Patrick Tierney • Abigail Thomas • Randolph Thomas • Joyce
Thompson • Andrew Toos • Patricia Traxler • Christine Turner • Kathleen
Tyau • Michael Upchurch • Daniel Wallace • Ed Weyhing • Joan Wickersham
• Lex Williford • Gary Wilson • Terry Wolverton • Monica Wood •
Christopher Woods • Celia Wren • Jane Zwinger

Our mother's mother's father,
Frank Davies, circa 1932.

Coming soon:

Gila opened the door and fell on top of her son who had fallen. When she landed, she found her face pressing into her son's chest and her knees twisted to the left of his hip. Her hands, which she had thrown out to break her fall, were firmly palming either side of his head. All in all it was not an awful fall. Just a strange one.

from "To Conjure the Twin" by Nomi Eve

Some women got onto me when I was writing about house-keeping, saying that that was regressive and anti-feminist ... Sure, I like having other options ... But that tradition, that lore, I think, is valuable. How to put a dress together without a pattern, how to cook this or that, how to iron, or how to hang a clothes-line. For instance, Ruth, my husband's mother, was a farmwife ... and couldn't waste a lot of time. So there was a way to hang a wash—or warsh, as she calls it—so you do the least amount of ironing and it dries quick ... Why would that be regressive?

from an interview with Julia Alvarez
by Mike Chasar and Constance Pierce

Sometimes good lines are not adding anything to a poem. You have them in there because you're enjoying your own skills, but it doesn't relate to the overall theme or the dramatic structure of the poem. Throw it out.

from an interview with Carolyn Kizer by Jim Schumock